MW01137404

Mystery of the Zodiac Killer

A Mandy and Roger Cozy Mystery
Book 5

Eleanor Kittering

This book is a work of fiction. All situations, characters and dialogues are part of the author's imagination. Although real locations may be referred to, they have no relation to any persons, living or dead and any resemblance is entirely coincidental. .

CONTENTS

CHAPTER ONE 1

CHAPTER TWO 9

CHAPTER THREE 19

CHAPTER FOUR 29

CHAPTER FIVE 39

CHAPTER SIX 51

CHAPTER SEVEN 59

CHAPTER EIGHT 69

CHAPTER NINE 77

CHAPTER TEN 85

CHAPTER ELEVEN 93

CHAPTER TWELVE 105

CHAPTER THIRTEEN 113

CHAPTER FOURTEEN 127

Be sure to get your FREE e-book "Suicide in Manhattan"
here:

http://bit.ly/2AEW7Hl

"Suicide in Manhattan" is a wacky romantic comedy set in
the 1950s about two late bloomers who fall in love while
trying to figure out life in general. A sweet clean romance.

You'll also be informed of when new books in the series
are going to be released.

Thank you, Eleanor Kittering

Eleanor Kittering

CHAPTER ONE

Eli Templeton decided to go to an estate sale that Sunday. He'd read about it Friday and thought that this might be an opportunity to find an unknown treasure that might be there. Eli was one of these history collectors that bought things at these sales as they struck his fancy. He didn't know an antique from a reproduction, but he knew what he liked and when he saw it, he bought it. A lot of these estate sales were just an opportunity for the owners to clear out the junk that somebody accumulated for decades, there were things that could be had for a song.

Finally arriving at the location, he found the house to be everything he had hoped for: a large type of old mansion that has run into difficult times, the type of environment that created great opportunities to find treasure. The keeper of the sale was at the door, an amiable and pleasant older man. Eli just told him "I'm just going to look around till I find something I like."

The estate keeper knew these types and welcomed them because he knew they bought any old junk thinking they found a great treasure. Once that junk was bought, it was one less thing to worry about.

"By all means take your time, hopefully you'll find something you like."

Eli wandered the place looking to see what jumped out at him. All of a sudden, there it was. A beautiful painting of a girl, looking as though it was from the 16th century or earlier. It appeared to be authentic, but sometimes these paintings were done at a later date to emulate an earlier time. Eli approached estate keeper and asked:

"How much do you want for that painting?"

The estate keeper looked at it, he couldn't wait to get rid of that eyesore.

"Give me two hundred dollars and it's yours."

Eli didn't hesitate "I'll take it."

They wrapped it in paper. Eli put it in the back of his car and drove away thinking that yes, life was good and he had found his treasure. In his mind, he would hang it in the living room and have something to look at while playing games.

Eli thought of his past. He had been an orphan his entire life, spending his childhood in an orphanage. Now that he was an adult, his only interests were video games and collecting old things. For some reason the old things gave him a feeling of security and purpose. Maybe because he had been abandoned, he felt these old things had been abandoned too and his obtaining them was his way of rescuing them from dying in oblivion. These relics were the orphans he had adopted, so they wouldn't be alone in life. Like him.

This painting resembled something that would eventually wind up in a land fill, but the girl in it was so lovely, he felt it would add elegance to the room. A big space in the living room of his house worked perfectly well with this painting. He knew sooner or later he'd find a picture for that space, and this was the perfect item.

Finally arriving home, he brought the painting into the living room. There was the bare wall that would benefit from the painting. He set about cleaning it first, removing as much dust as possible with a dust can. Then he drove the nails into the wall for the area where he thought the height would be best. He hung it up and looked at it. Now that it was spiffy, it actually looked very nice. It looked authentic, as though it was much older than he anticipated.

As he gazed upon the picture, he started to get dizzy. In his mind, he had fallen into a reverie. He felt as though the girl in the picture wanted to talk to him. He kept asking what do you want, are you ok? Then he came to the realization, he'd fallen in love with this girl, as though he's known her his entire life. Then she spoke to him.

"I need your help. I'm trapped in this picture. I can see you're a noble and handsome gentleman. With your help, I can leave this painting and live with you."

"Yes, of course I will help you. What can I do to get you free?"

"I knew the man I could love would come to my rescue. Follow my instructions and I'm sure we'll be together soon."

Eli was elated knowing that the girl in the picture had fallen in love with him too.

"Yes, of course. Tell me what you need."

"In the days to come I'll let you know. I can't wait to be free so I can be with you and we can love each other dearly."

Eli, comes out of the trance and goes back to his normal self, thinking that something had happened, but not exactly sure what it was. He looked at the picture on the wall and said, wow, that looks great. Then he thinks about fixing something for dinner then playing his favorite video game. After a couple of hours of playing, he gets tired and decides to go to sleep. He says, might as well, since I have to go work tomorrow.

Work consisted of being a floor clerk at the American Home Supply store at the mall. When he got there the next day, all through the morning, he felt as though he was in a fog. He felt that something important had happened, but couldn't remember what. He figured it had something to do with the video game. Perhaps a new challenge he forgot to set for himself. Sooner or later, he'd remember what it was.

He remembered when he got this job two years ago, thinking it was going to be a temporary job. He thought he might go to vocational school. But he couldn't quite make up his mind what he wanted to study. He thought he was still young, he had time. The orphanage had warped his mind so that he was still pretty much a teenager mentally, but he was approaching 30 soon.

He never had a real relationship with a girl, but he thought about getting a girlfriend, someday. The video games filled up the void in him. He felt empty most of the time, a great gaping hole inside of him. Inside the video game, he had a purpose, and he had friends. These were the other gamers he'd never met, but in the video game, everyone had a sense of purpose and unity. There was one girl that seemed to like him in the video game. At least, she tried to team up with him whenever she could. He didn't know where she lived though. He didn't want a long-distance relationship. He wanted someone he could see every day. He thought again, maybe in the future. It was always in the future, never in the present, and the present kept passing him by.

The day came to an end, it was time for him to go home again. He picked up some food on the way so that he wouldn't be interrupted while playing his video games. He figured he'd put in a couple of hours tonight. He racked up a lot of points recently, he was hoping to break his previous record. Or he could play that other game where that girl enjoyed teaming up with him. He thought about asking her where she lived. He felt very romantic these days and he didn't know why. He made a mental note to find out more about that girl in the next couple of days.

At one point, he could swear there was a voice in his head. The voice tells him:

"It's me Eli, the girl in the picture."

Eli seems to be transported to a different reality, he's really in a trance.

"Eli, we can be together, we can be in love. I'm so attracted to you. I feel you can understand me. But I have to get out of this painting for us to be together."

Eli can see the girl speaking to him in his mind, and she's more beautiful than ever.

"Please tell me what I need to do so that our union is soon."

"Oh, I knew I could depend on you, I knew you would be the one to save me. I need to get my life back. In order to do that, I need you to bring to me twelve young maidens. I will give you the power so you can select the right ones. When you bring me these maidens, I must borrow a little bit of their blood to build myself up. They won't miss it, but I will be fortified and I will be able to leave this painting. I need your help Eli, I'm so in love with you."

"Please tell me how to do this, I want to liberate you from this painting. I want you in my arms."

"As I do my love. Tonight, you can get the first one. When you go out to get her, you will know which one to get. You will feel she's the right one. Bring her to me and we'll start the process."

"Of course, when do I start?"

"We must wait for the cover of darkness to progress. Then you can go to a location you will see in your mind and there you will find the maiden."

Eli comes out of his trance and forgets everything that just happened. He goes back to playing the video game. Hours pass and he finds himself in a trance again. He hears the voice in his mind.

"It is time my love, you must find me the maiden."

"Of course, my lady. I will not fail you."

"You must wear a disguise so you cannot be recognized. Do you have something to conceal your face?"

Eli searched around the house, and found a ski mask.

"I think this will work."

"Yes, that will do."

Eli, leaves the house wearing the ski mask. He gets in his car heading for Main Street. It's a little past midnight and he gets there in no time. He parks the car, instinct telling him to stand by a certain corner. After fifteen minutes, there's a young woman that is coming his way. He hides in the shadows letting her pass a bit. He comes up from behind and starts to choke her. But not so hard as to kill her, just hard enough to cause her to lose consciousness. Once he's sure she's out, he drapes her over his shoulder and heads to his car. While he's in a trance, he gets all the information he needs to carry this out. He gets home and lays the woman in front of the picture.

"My lady, I have your first maiden."

"Wonderful, wonderful, I knew you were the man I had dreamed of all my life."

With the woman laid out in front of her, she proceeds to drain all the blood from the woman. After she's finished she speaks to Eli again.

"The exchange has happened Eli, you may bring her

back to the area where you found her. You'll know where to place her once you get there."

Eli picked up the now lifeless woman and drove back to the Main Street area. He walked with her on his shoulder again and at a point, he knew exactly where to place her. He laid her down on the ground, turned around and went towards his car, like an automaton. The trance controlled him completely.

Once he got home, he couldn't remember what he had done. He looked around the room, saw that the computer was on and continued to play video games. He looked at the time at one point and said to himself, "wow, how did it get so late, I better go to bed, otherwise I'll be a zombie tomorrow."

The woman in the picture said "Sleep, sleep my prince, tomorrow will be another day to get a new maiden."

Eleanor Kittering

CHAPTER TWO

The next morning, Mandy is doing a mental shopping list in her mind. She needs to buy cleaning supplies that they only sell at the American Home Supply store over by the mall. She figures she'll make a stop there and at the pet store as well. Get a couple of supplies for the cats.

Lana and Roger were sitting on the sofa, talking between themselves. Mandy comes over and talks to them.

"Hi my beautiful kitties. I am going to the store to get supplies. Roger, I'm putting you in charge of taking care of Lana keeping the house safe. I know you can understand me, so hopefully, this is something you can do."

Roger nodded and said "Listen, right now we're comfortable and we don't feel like going out. So you go do your errands and we'll be waiting for you right here when you come back."

All Mandy heard was a series of weird meows. She knew that Roger was talking but she couldn't understand him without the computer tablet.

"Not to complicate matters, I'm going to take that as a yes, Roger." And she laughed when she said it.

Roger nodded, to show it was ok.

Mandy left and got in her car. The mall wasn't that far away and it took her no time to get there. Once there, she found a parking space right away. As she walked towards the American Home Supply store, she remembered when she worked as a temp at the art gallery, a place no longer there. The reason it no longer existed there was because the owner was a murderer who almost killed her. She shuddered at the thought of that experience. She actually liked working at the place, till she discovered that the owner had killed his latest artist star. Such a terrible loss of life, she thought. She told herself "Mandy, stop thinking about the past, it's gone now. Let's focus on getting supplies for the house."

Once inside the store, she knew where she could find a cleaner that they only sold here. She walked down the aisle and sure enough, she found it. She also wanted to get a shelf for the bathtub area, so she could put stuff like shampoo and conditioner. She walked around and after a minute said to herself "I'm never going to find it like this, let me ask somebody." She found a man with the store t-shirt the employees wore. It was Eli.

"Hi there, how may I help you?"

"I'm looking for a shelf for the bathtub that you can stick on the tiles."

"Oh yes, that's in aisle 9A."

"Thanks very much."

"You're welcome."

And Mandy went to aisle 9A for her shelf. Eli continued on his way to tend to other customers.

Mandy left the store and proceeded to the pet store, for pet supplies.

"Oh hi Mandy, I see you're not bringing the cats along today?"

"No, I wanted to do quick jump at the mall and do some shopping. They seem quite put on the sofa and I didn't want to disturb them."

"Oh yes, I know all about that. When my Froodles sits down on that sofa, you couldn't move her with nitroglycerin. So I completely understand."

Mandy got the pet supplies she needed and left the store. She thought of going home directly but then she thought "Maybe I'll stop by the police station and say hello to Fred. We're supposed to get together tonight for our weekly dinner."

As she got closer to the police station, she saw a lot of commotion and activity, unusual for a Monday. She flagged one of the policemen she knew and asked what was going on?

"Hi Harry, what's all the activity."

"Found a murder victim this morning Mandy, a very strange case."

"A man or a woman?"

"A young woman, can't say much more than that."

"I understand Harry. I came by to say hi to Fred, but I'm sure this is not the best time."

"Yeah, I would hold off till later."

Mandy walked away concerned. Murders were rare in Pleasant Falls, she thought. A young woman found murdered? She'll ask Fred tonight when they have their dinner. She hoped that this wouldn't interfere with their dinner and he'd have to postpone it. Meanwhile, she decides to go to Joanie's and get a snack.

"Hi Mandy, haven't seen you in a while."

"I truly don't know why that is Joanie. I guess I'll have to come over more often."

"Where are those beautiful kitties?"

"Relaxing at home. When I was leaving, they seemed to be enjoying the sofa so much, they weren't much in the mood for travelling. So I figured I'd get some shopping done and check if they want to go to the park later."

"Yes, cats will be cats. Only doing the things they're in the mood to do."

"How about you Joanie, how have you been?"

"Well, you know that this place is my life. I just finished with the breakfast crowd and now I'm getting ready for lunch. It' seems quiet, but that's the calm before the lunch storm." Joanie laughed, knowing what was coming.

"I see, so I got really lucky that it's downtime now."

"You timed it when we were at our lowest ebb for the day."

"Well, I might be seeing you tonight with Fred. It all depends if he's not too busy. I passed by the police station and they were busy with some murder."

"Oh, that's awful. Hopefully it isn't someone I know, but I usually know so many people."

"I know what you mean Joanie. But Harry was very tight lipped, I didn't want to create a problem."

"Well, let's hope it's a solvable problem. Although, even if you catch the culprit, it doesn't bring back the victim."

"So true Joanie, so true."

After a little more chit chat, Mandy paid her bill and left. She had been looking forward to having dinner with Fred and now wondered if that would actually happen. She headed back to her car and headed for home.

She got home and was greeted by Lana meowing.

"Are you hungry honey? I brought treats."

"Lana, you're in luck she got you something."

"I guess you're interpreting what I told Lana, but it's for you too."

"Well, if Lana doesn't eat it, I will." Mandy just heard strange meows.

Mandy puttered around the house the rest of the day. During the afternoon, she decided to give Fred a call, to find out if he was going to make dinner.

"Hi Fred?"

"Hi Mandy, don't have much time to talk, we had a strange case today."

"I saw the commotion at the police station. Harry told me someone committed murder."

"Did he mention any details? They're not supposed to talk."

"No, just said it was a murder, that's why all the commotion."

"Harry's a good egg. He's usually not a blabber mouth."

"I was calling to find out if you still were able to make dinner tonight?"

"Oh yes, definitely. After today, I need to chill out, these are the days that drive you insane."

"Oh good, I was hoping I'd see you."

"Ok, I'll meet you at Joanie's?"

"Yes, let's meet at Joanie's."

Mandy thought to herself "Boy, this must have been some murder if they're so agitated."

Later that evening, Mandy headed over to Joanie's. Fred was already there.

"See Joanie, twice in one day. Can't say I haven't been coming over."

"Oh Mandy, you know you're always a part of this place. Fred's sitting over there."

Joanie pointed out the booth Fred was in.

"Hi Fred, nice to see you again."

"Same here Mandy. This place is a breath of fresh air compared to the day I've had."

"Sorry to hear that Fred, I won't ask about it, cause that may make you upset."

"Well Mandy, I'm going to mention it, because I may need your help later."

"Oh, why is that?"

"This doesn't fit into anything we know, and it may turn out to be something supernatural. You've been doing the astrology thing for a long time, it's possible you may have friends in other aspects of that field."

"I see. It's that strange, huh? What happened?"

"Well, one of my men were doing driving around town, keeping an eye on things and they find this woman lying on the sidewalk. At first it seems as though she may have fainted or something, she looked very pale. Turned out she was dead. Or so we thought. We called an ambulance and brought her over to the station for Joe the coroner to look at her.

"First thing he noticed, no rigor mortis. Even though she's supposedly dead, her limbs were supple. So Joe didn't want to do an autopsy, thinking this is a weird version of life and she was still alive. So, he tried to take a blood sample. Turns out she's been drained of her blood completely. She has no blood whatsoever. So, rigor mortis hasn't set in, she has no blood and she's technically dead. But seemingly alive too. We've never had anything like this before.

"This is why I say, it might be a supernatural thing. Ever since Roger started to talk, I've become very open minded about everything. I don't know what's going on here, but there's something that nobody, even experienced guys like Joe, have ever seen. So, we're keeping this under wraps now, but if you have any friends who may have ideas regarding this and can be discreet, I would be open to hear what they have to say."

"There's one woman I met in the past, she may have some answers, but off the bat, this may stump her as well. This doesn't sound like anything I've ever heard."

"Well, I'll keep you abreast of any developments. Let's order something to eat. I'm famished, didn't even have time for lunch."

"Yes, I think it's a good idea to stop talking shop and maybe focus on something more positive."

"I'm with you on that Mandy."

*****

Eli's night continued as usual. He looked forward to go home and play his video games. All day long he felt as though he was in a fog. He dealt with the customers as he usually did, but every time he had time to himself, he'd drift off into these fantasies of times gone by and saving damsels in distress, eventually snapping out of it and continuing his day at work, but it was hard for him to focus on the day.

His day at work finally finished and he got a sandwich before he went home. He thought of playing the game tonight where people work in teams. He hoped that one girl he played with would be playing tonight. He was going to try to find out more about her. He wondered if she lived nearby. You never know until you ask.

In the middle of playing his game, he started to drift into a trance. He heard a woman's voice calling.

"Eli? Eli, are you there?"

In his mind he could see the woman in the picture coming to life.

"Yes my lady, I am here."

"Oh, I've missed you today. Thank you so much for bringing me the maiden yesterday. I am beginning to get my strength back. Soon we'll be together and you can show me your world."

"I am so looking forward to that day. What is your name my lady?"

"I am Lucinda d'Avellaine, a princess."

Eli's heart jumped within him.

"You're a princess. That's amazing!"

"No, you're the amazing one, saving me from this picture."

"How soon before you're free?"

"Well, we'll have to borrow more blood from more maidens. Then I'll finally be strong enough for your world."

"When do we get another maiden?"

"Tonight would be good. The more maidens, the better."

"I will not fail you Lucinda."

"I am the luckiest girl in the world, having a man like you looking out for my interests."

"Oh no, it is I who am the lucky one."

"Well, we'll wait until the dark of night and capture another maiden, so I may borrow some of their blood."

"It shall be done Lucinda, it shall be done."

Right after this assertion on his behalf, he shakes his head and asks himself, what was I just doing? He looks at the computer and says, "Hey, I gotta get back to the game."

Eli continued playing the video game. He was very engrossed in killing as many of the enemy as possible that somewhere in the middle of that he stops as he hears a voice that says. "Eli, it's time."

He goes back to his trance mode and acts as though he is possessed. He puts on the ski mask, and walks out the door as though he's going to get a carton of milk. Meanwhile, in his head, he can clearly see where he has to go and what he has to do. He gets to Main Street again, stands at a certain corner. Young woman comes along, he grabs her and renders her unconscious. Carries her to the car and brings her back to the house. He engages in these actions, as though he's been doing this all his life, that's how controlled he is at this point.

Once at the house, he lays the woman before the picture. The blood is drained from the body and he is ordered to bring the woman back to the area where he found her. Afterwards he returns home.

Five minutes after, he becomes regular Eli again. He asks himself, what was I doing? He looks at the clock and asks says, wow, where does the time go? He considers going to bed, cause he knows if he gets back to the game, it's going to be hours of playing and it's pretty late already. As he goes across the living room, his eye catches the picture from the corner of his eye. He stops to look closer and says "You know, that's a very nice-looking girl. I wonder who she was?"

He continues to bed.

Eleanor Kittering

CHAPTER THREE

The next morning is yet another glorious morning in which the skies are blue and everything is right with the world. The town is quietly waking up and people are getting ready to go on their jobs and do the things that drive the mechanisms of an urban environment. A woman is walking her dog early that morning. She has her dog on one hand and on the other is her phone. She is skimming posts on social media, looking at what people have posted, how her different sites are doing and what her competition is doing. She's a blogger and although she has no real life, she has a lot of activity on social media. Keeping on top of the latest trends is her passion.

As she turns on to Main Street she notices that there is a woman lying on the street. She goes over to see what happened. She examines her up close and she doesn't seem to be breathing. She calls up 911. "Hi, I'm on Main Street and there is a woman here on the sidewalk completely immobile. I think that she's dead. Can you send someone over? It's at Main and Wooster."

After she calls in the dead woman, she starts live streaming her find.

"Hi everybody, this Brianna Morgan. I am livestreaming this disturbing find in my home town. I'm walking my dog this morning and I find this corpse just lying on the street. Now this is a strange occurrence in this little town, we really don't experience any murders. But to find somebody dead on the street is alarming."

All the while she's talking she's taking close-up shots of the woman on the streets, filming her from different angles, trying to see if there are any bruises that she can show to her "audience".

"Even though she appears to be dead, I'm not seeing any signs of violence. It's possible she had a stroke. Or maybe the attacker killed her in a way that didn't leave any marks. In any event, it's strange and I'm morbidly attracted to this situation. "

In the middle of this dialogue, the police arrive. They ask:

"Where's the body?"

She says, "right here" and walked over to it.

She continues filming and talking.

"The police have arrived and hopefully this woman can be taken to a hospital and see if there's something they can do help her or at least find the cause of death."

"Miss, are you taking pictures? You can't take pictures, this is a murder investigation right now, we can't have pictures."

"Oh, I'm not taking pictures, I'm filming the whole event."

"I have to ask you to please stop filming this. Not only is this a criminal investigation, there is respect for the deceased. It's not something to be shown as some kind of entertainment for your website."

"The people have a right to know. Why did this woman die? Are there others? What are the police doing to stop these deaths?"

"Miss, we don't know anything. She could have had a stroke, she could have had an existing medical condition that caused her to expire. Now, for the last time, I'm asking you, stop taking pictures and filming this procedure."

"I have a right to do as I please. I am the voice of the people. The people have a right to know."

Another policeman comes up from behind and grabs her phone and shuts it off.

"How dare you take my phone away from me! Give it back, give it back right now, I'm in the middle of an extraordinary reporting event."

"You'll get it back later at the police station. Right now, I'm asking you to leave, this is a police investigation. If you continue to intrude, I'm going to have to arrest you for the obstruction of justice."

"Obstructing justice! The people have a right to know what's going on, this is typical police brutality."

"Miss, I am advising you right now to walk away from here, and come by the station later to pick up your phone. Right now, we have to get this woman to hospital and find out what happened. All that you are interested in is getting more clicks on your website and raising your status on the internet. You couldn't care less if this woman lives or dies, you are trying to see if your video goes viral, because you are taking pictures of a corpse. Aside from being completely unethical, we are right now working and you are distracting us from doing our job. So please leave."

"I'll sue you for my phone. You can't talk to me this way. I wasn't doing anything wrong. It's within my rights to take pictures of whatever I want." While she's saying this she is walking away, dragging her dog behind her.

During this whole exchange, the ambulance has

arrived, one of the policemen says, "We better take her to the coroner, I think this one is like the one we picked up yesterday. That's two in a row so far. Fred is going to be interested in seeing this. "

Once at the police station, the woman is brought down to the coroner's office. He inspects her and says "Same thing as yesterday. I really hope this is not a trend."

Fred arrives shortly thereafter "Fred, we have another one of those corpses who is technically not dead, and technically not alive. Same thing, missing her blood, and no rigor mortis."

"I was hoping that yesterday's woman was a fluke, but now we have two in a row, I'm beginning to worry me that there are going to be more. Where was she found?"

"We found her at the same area we found the other, on Main Street."

"Well, keep this under wraps as well until we get an idea of what's happening."

"Fred, I got bad news. The woman who called it in starting livestreaming this the moment she found the corpse. I'm sure it's one of these internet idiots who is trying to get clicks on her videos and doesn't mind adverse publicity. She was fighting us and when we took her phone away, she threatened to sue the police."

"Great. So now, we have a video, no doubt graphically detailing the corpse up close and personal. The local news is sure to grab this and show that it happened on Main Street. Quincy will be coming down asking questions as to why we have a corpse on Main Street. Yes, this will turn into a circus. Meanwhile, Joe, keep this one on ice till we figure out what is going on, if there's a pattern and who is doing this. It's possible this may be a weird medical condition."

"Well, if it is, it's catching. So far, we've had two back to back."

"If we get another one tomorrow, we gotta start thinking it's some kind of serial killer, who is draining the blood from these women. I don't know how or why but we have the proof, it's happening and we don't know why."

Fred goes back to his office and turns on the local news, just to check if this has hit the news already. Sure enough, there it was.

"We are showing a video of a possible murder victim found on Main Street this morning. Authorities have not made any official statement whether this is a death or what is the cause, whether the woman died from natural causes or some kind of criminal activity."

"Well, so much for keeping this under wraps." Fred said to no one. At that moment his intercom rings.

"Fred, Quincy Wells is here to see you."

Quincy Wells had been the mayor of Pleasant Falls for the last twenty-five years. He was a man in his late 50s with graying hair. He was six feet tall and had to fight the battle of the bulge. So far, the bulge was winning. He wore the equivalent of a male girdle to keep himself looking as good as possible. He was up for re-election in a couple of months, and he worried over any negative events that happened in Pleasant Falls. A murder on Main Street is high on the list of those things that made Quincy Wells sweat bullets. Quincy walked into Fred's office.

"Fred, what is this? I saw on the news that there was a murder on Main Street today."

"Quincy, we're still investigating what happened to this woman. We don't know yet if it was a murder or if she has a medical condition. The unfortunate thing that happened is that the woman who found the body also used the situation as an opportunity to aggrandize her internet career and started to film the whole thing like it was a barbecue. Normally we want to keep these things under wraps. Right now, the official word is, we don't know if it's a murder or a medical condition."

"Well, I have to go on tv in a while, trying to do damage control. If my opponent gets wind of this, he'll be creating a counter campaign that I'm not keeping the streets safe and that people are dying on the streets as a result."

"I understand Quincy, but at the moment, we truly don't know what happened. There was no sign of violence and she has blood issues that we're investigating. That's why I say she may have died of a medical condition. Your best statement is that the police are not ruling this a murder, and they're investigating whether it's a medical condition."

"Ok, that's a ball I can run with. Anything else I should know of?"

"No, nothing else strange has happened. It's unfortunate that now everybody and their mother has a cell phone with a camera and video recorder and they feel they can share with the world whatever strikes their fancy. Whether or not it's ethical. If these phones didn't exist, this situation wouldn't have happened and there'd be time to investigate what is the real cause of death. Right now, the cause of death is a blood condition. Joe doesn't know what it is yet."

"Ok, I'll go with that the police are not ruling this a murder, and are investigating."

"That's the truth Quincy."

Quincy left feeling a little better that he didn't have a murder on his hands and a crime spree in town. He'll make a quick official statement to the press and hopefully that will quell any nasty scandals.

His nephew, Taylor Wells was waiting for him at the car. Taylor was in his mid-twenties, dark brown hair 6 feet tall. Although not the most ambitious guy in the world, people liked him because he had a nice personality and was generally a good person. Taylor was doing odd jobs for Quincy in the guise of a job. Right now, he was driving him around town to his different meetings.

"So, what happened Uncle Quincy?"

"Well, the good news is Fred says it doesn't appear to be a murder, so that's a relief."

"What does he think it is?"

"Says it could be a medical condition. All I know is that now I don't have to worry that we have a murderer in town. That could be ammunition for my opponent, who will turn around and say that I'm letting murderers run around loose on the streets. Politics is so dirty Taylor. Whatever you do, don't get into it. Get a nice job working for a company, where you don't have to constantly be dealing with the public."

"So, why did you take the job Uncle?"

"Well, back when I was young and idealistic, I thought I could make a change for the better. The trouble is, not everybody defines better the same way you do, so when I thought I was making improvements to the town, others did not think that they were improvements. And so on. So, in the end, being the mayor is a pretty thankless job, but it's a job I know I can do, and I truly do like the people of this town, so I continue to try to improve life and hopefully that works for everybody."

"So, is there any chance I could get a job in one of the many government offices?"

"Well Taylor, that's why I'm giving you these odd jobs for now. Until I get re-elected, it's not a good time to give out jobs, especially to family members, because then my opponent will criticize me for giving jobs to those not qualified or nepotism or both. Again, politics is a dirty business. But when this blows over, and I'm re-elected, I'll hook you up with an internal job."

"Thanks uncle."

After Taylor dropped off his uncle at the mayor's office, he went to visit his girlfriend, Natalie Martin, who worked at the local tv station. Natalie was in her mid-twenties, blonde and attractive. She looked good on tv, a medium where she was trying to get a career in. He was going to meet her for lunch. She was waiting for him outside.

"Hi there. How's my favorite tv news anchor?"

"Well, I'm not a news anchor yet. I'm lucky they gave me that slot "Could it be True?" where I interview weirdos with unusual theories about life. Hey, what's this about a murder on Main Street?"

"Well officially, it's still under investigation, but it appears to be a medical condition. That's what the cops are saying. Truth is they don't know. So far, it doesn't appear to be a murder."

"Yeah, the station was upset that the rival station got to it first. That's the thing today, people put stuff up on the web, and depending on who's on the lookout for stories on the web, larger studios grab the story. Finding stories on the web is Marcia's job and she called out sick today. So, they're not too happy with her. And she calls out sick a lot. So, unhappiness is ongoing."

"Well, I'll keep you posted if of any further developments."

"Yeah, I just gotta catch a break, finding a real news story that will keep people coming to their tv or web page over and over. And so far, that hasn't happened."

"Well, look, at least you got a job, me I'm still sending out resumes."

"I think we both gotta start looking in Manhattan. The job market is not that good in this area of New Jersey."

"Yeah, I'm going to try that and see if that starts happening. At least my uncle says once this election is over, he'll get me a job."

"What if he doesn't get elected?"

"He always gets elected. The people love him. He might be a little goofy from time to time, but he's been honest, never robbed anybody and he's tried to take care of the people's need. Every time re-election comes around he gets all nervous that he's not going to get elected. And then they elect him. I'm not worried. So, are you hungry, where do you want to eat?"

"Let's go over to the mall and get a burger or something, I gotta get back for a meeting."

"Ok, let's go."

Back at the police station, Fred was beginning to get worried. He said to himself, two murders in two days, both exactly the same. What is going on here? Nobody knows how they are doing this. In his mind he thought of asking Roger. Has it come to this? He's asking a cat for advice? He hoped that there wasn't a third cause otherwise, he had a real crisis on his hands. Today, he was able to stave off Quincy. But if there's another murder and it's the same, people are going to say that there's a serial killer, and honestly, it has the earmarks of that. But to himself, he didn't want to say that. Cause he'd have to admit that things are much worse than they are right now. And they were pretty bad.

The phone rang and it was Mandy. "Hi Fred, I was going over to Joanie's for lunch, I was wondering if you wanted to join me?"

"Normally Mandy, I would love to but believe it or not, we had another one of those murders again."

"You mean the one with the blood drained."

"Exactly the same. Mandy, I don't know what to do. Nobody knows what to make of this. If you can put your feelers out in the supernatural community as to what could be doing this, I would appreciate it. There's supposedly a mythical creature called the Chupacabra out in Puerto Rico. But in New Jersey? Highly unlikely. Anyway, this thing supposedly sucks the blood out of people. If you can look that up, I'd be very grateful. Right now, I just have too much on my plate."

"Sure Fred, I understand. I know one person that I'm sure I can reach out to and I'll do research on the Chupacabra and see if there's any relation to what's going on."

"Thanks so much Mandy. Maybe tonight we'll get together."

*****

Later that night, Eli was playing his favorite video games, having a good time actually. It was getting very late. All of a sudden, as though something took over him, he stopped playing the video game. He heard the voice.

"Eli, I am getting stronger, but I still need to borrow more blood from young maidens. Will you help me tonight? I can't wait till this process is over and you and I can be together."

"Of course I'll help. Let me know where I can find a new maiden and I'll bring her over."

"You'll know exactly which to select my love. When she appears, you'll know what to do."

"I will not fail you.."

"It's only a matter of time now Eli, soon we'll be together.

After this exchange, in the midst of a trance, he leaves the house to engage in his nightly mission.

CHAPTER FOUR

Another morning brought another day at Pleasant Falls. Natalie Martin had been wondering what she could do to get more visibility on the station. She decides to approach the producer and see if he'll let her interview the woman who found the body yesterday. Maybe there's a story there, maybe not. But since this woman was livestreaming this, she probably is trying to get some a reputation online for reporting the local news or something.

The way she's going to try to sell the story to the producer is that yes, the competing station got the video first but, we can interview the woman who took the video and she can tell us what her impression is about encountering the dead body. Whereas other people have seen a video, we're getting the scoop on the person that posted it. Something told her to do a little more investigation on the woman before she presented this though.

She went on the web and looked up the woman: Brianna Morgan. She had a website dedicated to all kinds of things. Apparently, whatever struck her fancy. She read her story about yesterday's events. She read a lot of other stories on the website. She started to have second thoughts about interviewing this woman. She sounded a lot like the nuts that she regularly interviewed on her spot "Could it be True?" The difference was that it was all trashing the local politicians, police and businesses in Pleasant Falls. This could backfire on her if it's seen as she is supporting somebody who is against the community. Oh, why was it so hard to get a real good story?

She turned on the tv to the news of the rival station. Apparently, Steve Tyrell, the man running against Quincy Wells, had an announcement to make to the press. Why was he going to them and not to her station? We would have supported him, she tells herself. She sat back and decided to listen to what he had to say.

"Ladies and gentlemen, I come to bring a public service announcement. It has come to my attention that there is a serial killer loose in Pleasant Falls. So far, has attacked and killed three women in Pleasant Falls. And why don't you know about it. Because the police department has been covering up this debacle so that it doesn't interfere with the election plans of my opponent, Quincy Wells.

"You would think a man that has been mayor of this town for 25 years would make the safety and welfare of the citizens of this town a priority by making an announcement to stay indoors to be safe. But no, he has been hiding this information so that the voters aren't aware of his incompetency. Quincy Wells has hidden this from you ladies and gentlemen.

"If elected mayor, I would never hide this from the general public, I would advise them to stay indoors until this murderer is caught and brought to justice. Three dead women ladies and gentlemen in the space of three days.

We got the information from the grieving families, who have not been allowed to see the corpses of their daughters. We have a right to know ladies and gentlemen, what the police are doing and what that means for the citizens of this town. The three women are the following: Elaine Merkel, Jennifer Scott and Elizabeth Waring. All of them young women who needed our protection and who we failed to protect. And now, they are the honored dead. "

Natalie was dumbstruck. A serial killer? Why didn't she get this information? And how did Steve Tyrell get this information? Obviously, he must be looking for dirt in all the right places. Natalie calls Taylor.

"Taylor, have you heard the news."

"No, I haven't, I was just having breakfast."

"Well, apparently there's a serial killer in Pleasant Falls and Steve Tyrell is saying that your uncle has been hiding this from the community."

"What! No way. I would have heard uncle talking about this yesterday. Believe me, a serial killer would have put my uncle through the roof and I would have heard about it."

"Well, either Steve Tyrell is really pushing the boundaries of fake news, or something has happened recently that seems to be a serial killer."

"Listen, I gotta get off. My uncle is on the other line, I'm sure he wants me drive him somewhere."

"Let me know if you get any real strong dirt on this. My station is going to be ballistic for missing this story."

"Taylor, have you heard the news?!"

"Natalie was just telling me about it."

"I need you to drive me pronto to the police station. Fred Stone has a lot of explaining to do."

"Yes sir, I'll be right there."

Taylor thought no use trying to discuss the subtleties of what may have happened, or if this is some recent development. When his uncle got upset, you couldn't reason with him. Let's find out what this is really all about, Taylor thought. He found Quincy standing outside the mayor's office. He got in the front.

"I just can't believe that this has been happening under my nose and my own police department didn't tell me about it."

"Well, Fred's a sensible guy, I'm sure there's a good explanation why."

"A serial killer. This is the last thing I needed. My ratings are going to go through the basement."

"Well, let's see what we find out."

There was a large group of people standing outside the police station. A couple of news stations were parked outside, waiting for a word from the police about the recent statements about a serial killer. Quincy made his way through the crowd, heading into the police station. There were policemen outside the police station keeping out the various people who wanted answers outside.

"Harry, I'm here to see Fred."

"Go right in Mr. Mayor."

Quincy stormed into the police station and demanded to see Fred.

"Fred is downstairs in the morgue, along with the doctors and coroner."

Quincy went downstairs with Taylor tagging along.

"Fred, why wasn't I told that there was a serial killer in town. The town is in a mass panic over this, wondering what are we doing to protect."

"Quincy, I don't know who leaked this story, but they don't have all the facts, and basically, they're spreading fear and panic for the sake of attention."

"Well, why don't you tell me the facts Fred. I'm going

to become the laughing stock of this town for not protecting them from a serial killer."

"Calm down Quincy. First of all, I want to introduce you to Dr. Howard and Dr. Zeissburg, both from the state hospital. They specialize in abnormal pathology and biology. The reason why I haven't made a statement or bothered to tell you is because, we don't know what were dealing with here. So far, we've had three victims, the latest from early this morning. She was found on Main Street which is where we have found all the victims.

"The reason we have called in the doctors, is because Joe, our coroner, doesn't know what's happening here and neither do these gentlemen who have been kind enough to try to help with this dilemma. The problem is Quincy, these women are found drained of all their blood. There are no puncture marks, there is no sign of violence. You would think they were dead, but no, in some way we cannot explain, they seem to be alive as well.

"There is no criminal who is capable of doing this Quincy, at least not a human criminal, and it's certainly not animal criminal. So yes, the victims seem to turn up daily, but nobody knows how they get in that state. We have combined medical experience here of almost 80 years Quincy and they've never seen anything like this in their lives. So, this is why I didn't tell you, and didn't make a public statement. The families are understandably upset why we haven't let them see their daughters, or tell them what happened. But Steve Tyrell got wind of this, went to them and preyed on their sympathy. That guy is a vulture Quincy.

"So, as far as we can tell, there is no "serial killer" in the classic sense of some deranged individual killing people. But something is happening to these women. We're trying to find out Quincy, but it's going to take time. This is why I kept a lid on it. Now the cat's out of the bag and that's not a good thing."

"But what am I going to tell the people Fred? They're out there angry that this is happening and that we're not doing anything to stop this."

"Quincy, we go and we tell them the truth. First, I state quite clearly that there is no evidence of a serial killer. However, we found a couple of women who seemed to have been found dead, but who are not dead, but in some kind of coma. There is no sign of violence perpetrated on these women. We leave out the part that they're missing their blood otherwise they're going to go ballistic."

"Ok, that sounds like a plan. And I'll accuse Steve Tyrell of creating mass hysteria by not having any of the facts, just some stories from the families of the women affected."

"That's good Quincy, throw this guy under the bus."

Fred and Quincy left the morgue and headed outside. A crowd of people we're outside the police station as well as news stations with their trucks. They asked for people to quiet down as they had an announcement to make. Quincy started things off.

"Ladies and gentlemen, recently you may have heard from Steve Tyrell information that there is a serial killer loose on our streets. That is simply not true and Steve Tyrell should be ashamed of himself for spreading false information. I have Captain Fred Stone here from our own Pleasant Falls police department who would like to make a statement as to what is really happening."

"Thank you, Mayor. Recently we've come across some victims in town that upon our first finding them, they appeared to be dead. We've been finding one every day for the last three days. However, upon closer examination, these women are still alive and they seemed to be in a very strange coma. We've invited medical professionals to study and inspect these women and possibly find out what is wrong with them. At present, they don't know, but we feel it's some kind of medical condition. We're trying to find out if this is chemically induced by some of the local factories. In light of this, they're being moved to a local hospital for further testing.

"Allegations of a serial killer are simply not true, and please do not listen to any sources out there, since no one, but the police department is investigating this phenomenon, and we have medical specialists who are working with us. Again, I would like to reiterate, there is no maniac out there committing horrible crimes upon the population of Pleasant Falls. However, if you see someone lying on the street, seemingly dead, please call the police right away and let us handle this. Something is going on, but it's not criminal activity. "

"Thank you, Captain Stone. People of Pleasant Falls, as your mayor, you know that I would never willingly do anything to put the lives of the people in danger. Steve Tyrell, my political opponent, has been creating mass hysteria in an effort to undermine my abilities as mayor. As Captain Stone has said, there is no serial killer, but we do have a strange situation.

"This is a time where I ask each and every one of you to look out for each other. If you see somebody feeling faint or somebody feeling ill, please do not hesitate to call the police. It's possible if we catch these victims in the early stages of whatever is happening, we may be able to learn what is causing this and to stave off other cases in the future.

"We have the cooperation of some great medical minds who are trying to figure out what is going on here. But please do not give in to fear and panic based on statements that are simply not true. The only reliable source for news regarding this situation in the future is our local police department, since they have the situation under control."

There was some mild applause and the people felt generally better about things since now it appeared to be a medical condition. This left some people concerned but by the same token, since nobody had an answer, so they felt better at not being the only clueless ones.

Fred and Quincy went back inside to further discuss the issue.

"Listen Fred, I want you to keep me in the loop of this as it progresses. I think we managed to stave them off for now, but you know how people are, they are more willing to believe in a serial killer than some kind of medical condition. So far, this has affected three women, one every day. If we find another tomorrow, we gotta start looking as to who might be causing this. I just don't believe that people are dropping dead, and then they're not dead, but they're missing all their blood."

"I agree with you Quincy. And you know that this guy Steve Tyrell is not going to take this lying down. He's going to strike by working the fear aspect, since that always gets people's attention."

"Yeah, he's from the Steve Lombardi school of politics, winning isn't everything, it's the only thing. And he wants to win without caring how he does it."

"Well Quincy, I'm working on this round the clock. Sooner or later we're bound to find out what's causing this."

"Ok, let me know if you find anything Fred."

"I will."

Quincy left Fred's office and him and Taylor left the building. Taylor drove Quincy back to mayor's office. He called Natalie to fill her in.

"Hey, did your tv station go down to the police station."

"For once, they also got in on the news. So, I saw the whole statements from Quincy and Fred. The local papers however, have afternoon editions talking about the serial killer. It's still strange that women are supposedly dying, not dying and it's a new one every day."

"I was down in the morgue when they were talking to the doctors and the doctors were baffled. So, if they're baffled, what hope is there for the rest of us."

"Well, let's hope that there are no more victims for a while. Maybe the whole thing is a fluke."

"Yeah, let's hope no one else gets afflicted, if that's what it is."

And they hung up. Meanwhile Jack Connor, a local ufologist, contacted one of the stations with his take on what's going on. They interviewed him on the street.

"I listened today to what the Mayor and the police captain were saying about the victims and it sounds very much like alien abduction. Particularly, this is more reminiscent of cattle mutilations, without the mutilations. Maybe the aliens are using more humane technology to do tests and experiments on their subjects. This is why there is no trace of violence. If more victims disappear in the days to come, this is definitely a full-blown alien invasion. They're just getting subjects now to find our weaknesses."

"But why are they just taking women?"

"Well, maybe they're not too informed on our culture and figure that if women are responsible for giving birth, maybe they're figuring out a way of creating an artificial womb to create human clones that they can enslave."

"I see. Well, thank you very much Jack for sharing your views on the possible cause of this recent crop of events. "

And they signed off. Mandy was watching this on the tv, and was shaking her head at how whenever something like this happens, all the nuts come out of the woodwork.

CHAPTER FIVE

Mandy had gone to the mall briefly and picked up a couple of things. She found an afternoon edition of the local paper out, and she got a copy. The headline read "Serial Killer in our Midst: Who's next?" Once home she perused the paper and looking at their version of the story. They had a list of the women so far "killed" by the serial killer and their dates of birth and death. And then one thing leapt out at her. The zodiac signs of each woman followed in strict succession. Somebody was draining the blood of these women deliberately following the order of the zodiac signs. She called Fred.

"Hi Fred."

"Hi Mandy. Hopefully, you caught the segment this morning on tv?"

"Yes, definitely seemed to placate to the townspeople."

"So, you have any other ideas."

"Actually, something very important just leapt out at me, and it came from reading The Daily Rag."

"Oh yes, somebody brought in a copy. I saw they're still following the serial killer angle."

"Fred, I hate to say this, but there may be something to that and here's why. You have three victims so far. The paper listed their dates of birth and deaths. Each one of the victims is of a different zodiac sign, but in strict succession. So, whoever is doing this, is doing this according to the zodiac and which means there are going to be twelve victims. And another thing Fred, this is definitely a supernatural act. Somebody is doing something very strange and draining those women of their blood. Whenever someone does this in the supernatural, they do it for some ritual to gain power. Blood has always been the fluid of choice for sacrifices. It's possible these women are some type of sacrifice for some purpose."

"Well Mandy, this doesn't make it any easier."

"I know, but you can expect another victim tomorrow and if what I'm seeing is right, she's going to be the zodiac sign Cancer, the fourth sign Fred."

"Let's hope you're wrong, but if you're right, I got a serial killer on my hands."

"Exactly. Fred, you know I try to be as even keeled as possible but sometimes the only possible explanation is the strange one. Unfortunately this time, it's a supernatural situation, but I'm not familiar enough with it to give you some hard answers."

"Well, please look into it and see if anybody in the supernatural community has an idea what kind of sacrifices or rituals they're doing requiring the blood of an individual and how can they do so without any incision."

"I'll ask around and see what I can dig up. Usually the clues come out of left field, like with the paper and the zodiac signs."

"Right now, we've moved these women to a special ward at the hospital. Apparently, they don't need to be chilled to be preserved, there's no rigor mortis and no rotting is taking place, but the doctors prefer if they were monitored in a medical facility. Also, it makes it easier for the families to go visit."

"That's good. Better than being kept in a morgue. I'll see what I can find."

"Great. I'll have to get off, since I still have a large group of people who are still asking questions."

"Yeah, I'm sure that's something that's not going to go away easy anytime soon."

*****

Steve Tyrell was not giving up so easily. He smelled a rat and a cover up, and yes something strange was going on, but he knew there was more to this than that. He figured, wait for the next victim before making his next announcement. He speculated on someone close to these women so he could get more inside information? The news said the women were being moved to the hospital. Steve bet one hundred dollars in his mind somebody at the hospital was open to a bribe to find out what the state of the women were. He reached out to his campaign manager, Tracy Reeves.

"Tracy. Steve here."

"Hi Steve, sorry the expose didn't go off quite as we had planned. Quincy covered his bases pretty much."

"Yeah, I still smell a rat. There's something here still that doesn't add up. I know they're saying the women in a coma, but are they truly in a coma? I heard they moved them to the hospital. We need to pay somebody off to find out what is the condition of these women, is there anything strange with these women, other than they're supposedly in a coma."

"That might be simpler than you think. There are nurses' aides and people who are doing a lot of work at the hospital and not getting paid adequately who wouldn't mind making a couple of hundred bucks extra. Leave it to me, I'll find somebody to go investigating."

Tracy asked her volunteers to see if anybody knew anybody at the hospital.

"Listen, we have a situation where we feel Mayor Wells was not entirely telling the truth regarding these women. Does anyone here have a friend or family member who works at the hospital who can look into the condition of the women being held there? We'll pay them a nice little bonus for information."

"My cousin works there as a nurse's aide. She hates the job but she needs the money."

"Well, do you think your cousin would be interested in making a couple of hundred bucks for finding out what state the women brought from the police department are in?"

"I can ask. If she has access to them, I'm sure she'll do it."

"Can you call her now, time is of the essence."

"Sure, let me try."

The volunteer called her cousin.

"Hi Wendy?"

"Hi Rachel, what's up?"

"Listen, we're concerned the mayor wasn't really telling the truth about those women being found around town in a coma. They brought them to the hospital this afternoon. Can you find out if there's anything strange other than the obvious? You can make $200 bucks, doesn't matter what you find out, if it's good or bad."

"Sure, I can ask around and see what's going on there."

"Can you do it tonight?"

"I'm pretty sure I can go by that floor and ask some

questions."

"Ok, get back to me if you get any information."

"Well Tracy, now we wait till she comes back with something. I told her $200 dollars, is that ok."

"That's perfectly fine Rachel, any information is very helpful."

Tracy thought to herself 'It's not my money and any information is better than no information. We can't go out on a limb again like we did this morning. That could definitely backfire on us.'

After a couple of hours, Rachel got a call back from Wendy.

"Hi Wendy, did you learn anything?"

"Actually, I think I did, but it sounds so weird, I don't know if it's right."

"That's ok, listen, I'm going to put you on speaker so Tracy can hear this as well."

Rachel motioned for Tracy to come over.

"Hi Wendy, it's Tracy. I wanted to thank you so much for your help and believe me, good or bad, you'll get paid for helping us out."

"Well Tracy I don't know if this is of much help, but I talked to one of the family members and she told me something very strange."

"What is it Wendy?"

"She said none of the women have any blood. Something drained the blood out of them. Nobody knows why or how."

"Really? Anything else."

"Nothing more, other than she was happy now she was able to visit because she worried her daughter was getting worse. But that's all I got."

"Wendy that is a big help. You come by tomorrow and I'll pay you in cash."

"Thanks, I appreciate it."

Rachel hung up the phone and asked Tracy "What does it mean?"

"It means they held out on the public. Yes, the women are in a supposed coma, and they're looking into it, but blood. Blood gets people crazy. Drained of their blood? Sounds like vampire stuff and the kind of stuff we can use to get back at Quincy. So this is very good. Thank you Rachel for having a cousin who worked at the hospital."

"You're welcomed.

*****

Later that night, Eli was playing his video game. He was on a team with the girl he liked and who seemed to like him. Apparently, she lived in Pennsylvania, which was not far from New Jersey. He was working up the courage to go visit out there. Nothing heavy or big, just go out there and hang. Meet in the real world as opposed to the world of games. That was the thing about games, they allowed you to be in that world for hours and hours, days even. It was so real, you lost track of time and track of your life. Which was one of the reasons he enjoyed games so much. In the games, he was able to be whoever he wanted and he was in touch with these people, the other players. In his regular life, he didn't have any friends and nobody that understood him. He'd chat with this girl out in Pennsylvania and they had things in common. She was 23. He was 28, so it wasn't a situation where he was 40 and she was 15, nothing crazy like that. They were close in age. He had been thinking a lot of late about that girl. She seemed to reach out to him in the game, which is why he had the courage to even speak to her in the first place. Normally he couldn't bring himself to do even that.

Then he heard the voice in his mind.

"My love, are you ready to get me another maiden?"

In a moment, Eli became this other person, controlled by the voice in his head.

"Yes Lucinda, I am counting the days when you and I can be together."

"As I am my love, as I am. Now is a good time, as the dark of night is upon us."

"I shall leave now."

Eli went through the setup of going out, putting on the ski mask and wearing gloves so as not to leave prints. He returned to Main Street, since that's where he would find the next woman to offer to the picture. Cassie Harrison was walking home after her shift as a waitress at the diner she worked. But she wasn't tired, she was a night owl. She loved walking at this time of night since she had Main Street to herself. She was enjoying the night air, when suddenly Eli came out of the shadows. She jumped quickly to one side and said "Hey, are you trying to give me a heart attack, what's wrong with you anyway?"

Eli didn't talk in this state. He attempted a grab for the girl. Cassie had been taking self defense lessons for two years now, mostly as exercise and also because you never know. She thought this was one of those you never know times. As Eli got close, she did a flying leap and kicked him in the face. She landed on her feet ready for battle. Because the trance state gave Eli great physical strength, he didn't even flinch when she kicked. He heard a voice in his head that said "Hit her hard."

He feinted with his left arm and she tried to defend herself. That was a ruse which left her open to get punched in the jaw. He hit her so hard, he knocked her out immediately and she hit her head on the ground when she fell. Satisfied she was unconscious, he took her over his arm and brought her back to the house. After the process was over, he brought her back to Main Street.

However, it was clear Cassie had been in a fight. She just laid there, the blood drained from her body.

*****

In the morning, an older lady was walking her dog. She came upon Cassie's body. She took a picture with her phone, and uploaded it to her social media page. She had been deeply affected by the recent events of the women being found on the street. After she put up the picture with the caption "Is this another victim?" she called the police.

The police came right away and immediately knew this was yet another victim of the same as the others. They noticed she was a little beat up. Half an hour later, the news was abuzz that yet another victim had been found, making it the fourth so far. The picture online showed this one had been in a fight.

Steve Tyrell announced in a video here was yet another victim, and it had come to his attention all these women had been found drained completely of their blood. This fourth woman shows she was involved in a struggle, which confirms what I had said yesterday, we have a serial killer among us and nobody is taking any action to stop him.

Quincy ran down to the police station wanting to talk to Fred.

"Fred, what happened? How did Steve find out the women were drained of the blood?"

"Once at the hospital, I can't control who opens their mouth. They probably asked around till somebody talked. Steve is looking for dirt, and he usually finds it."

"Yes, but since this announcement, my ratings are going down, we gotta say something to evade this storm."

"There's nothing we can say Quincy. I was summoned, just like you, made aware of this new woman."

Quincy and Fred went downstairs to the morgue. Fred

asked.

"Well Joe, what's the story. Does she fit the pattern the others?"

"She does, in the sense her blood is drained. There was definitely a struggle with this one, as though she was fighting someone off. She was hit here and she has a sizable bump on the head, probably from when she hit the ground from the fight. Somebody is definitely doing this Fred, I just don't know how."

"Did she have any ID? A driver's license."

"They found her things as usual, nothing missing in her personal effects."

Fred put on a pair of gloves and looked at the license. He looked to see when she was born.

"Yeah, she checks out, another young woman, similar in age."

"Fred, it's great you're seeing a pattern, but what am I going to tell the people out there. I'm sure by now there's a crowd gathering outside."

"We'll have to make a statement. Let's go and do it, so we can get back to figuring out who did this."

Fred and Quincy headed for the area outside the police station. There was a crew of local news and film crews waiting for them.

"Mr. Mayor, can you explain the allegations that these women are being drained of their blood?"

"Mr. Mayor, is this a serial killer who's doing this? Who is doing this?"

Quincy called for order and quiet.

"Ladies and gentlemen, I am sorry to have to announce we have another victim, the fourth in four days. We do not know why these events are happening or if there is a who doing this. All we know is she follows the same pattern as the other women. Yes, she has been drained of her blood and we don't know how or why that is happening either. We have doctors looking into this and they can't explain it either. So, in summary, we're not holding out on you. It's just this case is so remarkable, we are at a loss as to what to call this."

"Mr. Mayor, is this be the work of a serial killer, using very sophisticated tools."

Fred answered that one.

"So far, we have no evidence these acts are being perpetrated by a human being."

"What about the work of aliens? Jack Connor said aliens are abducting these women for experiments."

"No comment. Again, I am sorry but that is all we have for you today. I wish we had more, but we are trying hard to understand this and put a stop to it."

Fred and Quincy returned inside, leaving behind a clamor of people who wanted more answers.

"Fred we gotta put a stop to this. Not only is the town terrified, but people are losing their faith in me."

"Quincy, you know I want this stop as much as you do. But we're up against a brick wall."

"Let me know if anything else develops the moment you know it."

"I will Quincy, I will."

Once Quincy left Fred's office, Fred called Mandy.

"Hi Mandy, by now you probably heard the latest."

"Yes, they found another woman."

"This is her date of birth."

"She's born under zodiac sign Cancer, Fred. That's the fourth sign. She's the fourth victim"

"I was hoping you wouldn't say that. I'm truly at a loss

as to what to do."

"I'm sure you'll eventually come up with something. We know this much, these women aren't draining their own blood. Someone or something is doing this. If I figure out anything Fred, I'll let you know. But in the end, this will get resolved. But it's going to be weird."

CHAPTER SIX

Roger and Lana are talking. Or rather Roger is talking and using Lana as a sound board for ideas running through Roger's mind.

"I've been hearing Mandy talking to Fred about these murders and now she's saying there's a certain logic with the zodiac, and a guy is draining the women's blood, I gotta say, as crazy as it sounds, this is exactly what a psychopath does. Don't know why he does it, but this sounds to me like a serial killer who is completely and utterly crazy. The question is now, how do we stop him?

"From what Mandy is saying, he gets his victims and then he drops them in the middle of town. Minus their blood. Nobody knows how he does this. So, it's possible the supernatural is involved. Or perhaps a new technology not everybody is savvy to.

"Well Lana, I gotta get involved because I know I can help. But what's to say Fred wants my help? I'm sure the last thing Mandy wants is for me to get involved tracking a serial killer. She'll be worrying if I get hurt. Meanwhile, who has saved her in the past from these other killers?

Me, that's who. So, I can't let sentimentalism get in the way of solving a crime."

"Yes, but Roger, a lot of this would make sense if they saw you as a man. But as a cat, how are you going to get around? How are you going to ask questions? And how are you going to catch the killer?"

"You definitely have valid points Lana. This being a cat situation stinks, not offense. Last time I worked in conjunction with Fred, that project worked. I was able to weaken the killer while Fred arrested him and you hissed like crazy at the woman. This time, we don't know who the killer is, and unlike the last guy, he is engaged in gruesome stuff."

"I remember that hissing incident. I never want to do that again. However, you could ask Mandy that you want to work with Fred and she will probably ask him."

"The thing is, from what I hear of Mandy and Fred talking, he really is under a lot of stress to find this killer. He may not be as open minded to having me help him out. People are definitely funny about certain things, I can tell you from experience of being a man.

"Back in the day, when I was a full-time cop, if someone suggested I take a cat as a partner, I would not be overjoyed as the prospect. I'm sure Fred probably feels the same way. So, that's why I'm not asking Mandy to ask Fred.

"But I also feel my hands are tied. This is something that I am good at and I can make a difference for the good. Believe me, I am not very happy to learn that various women have died at the hands of a psychopath. It makes me want to run out all over town until I find the guy and bring him to justice. But I gotta plan this out in a very methodical manner to maximize my strengths as a cat."

"Somehow, I think you'll wind up hurt in this ordeal

Roger."

"That's a chance you're always taking as a cop. But if you save somebody's life in the course of taking action, it's worth it. "

"Well, let's hope they don't kill any other women."

"According to Mandy, the killer's goal is twelve. He only has four, he has eight more to go."

"Oh." Lana said with a small voice, realizing things were much serious than she thought.

"I'm going to have to see if an opportunity presents itself."

Meanwhile, in another part of town, another drama was unfolding.

"Uncle Quincy, I feel like deadwood these days. I went to college, I come back to this town and I still can't get a job. I thought that in a small-town area like this I could find a job, but no. Isn't there anything in the government you could hook me up with."

"Like I said before Taylor, it's an election year, and giving you a job could be viewed as nepotism and that I hired my nephew over another qualified candidate."

"I mean, a big reason I came back is to be close to Natalie. Me and her have been going out now for a while, but she at least has a job as a newscaster. I don't want to look like a bum."

"I hear you Taylor, it's hard being young. And I'd really try to help you, but right now, in addition to this being an election year, we have this serial killer on the loose in Pleasant Falls. The people are looking to me to get rid of this menace and so far we don't have anything on this monster."

"Ok, here's a question for you Uncle Quincy. If I solve this serial killer mystery, could you get me a job with the town?"

"Taylor, if you solve this mystery, I'll make you the police captain."

"The police captain, you mean it!?"

"I mean it Taylor. But be careful, this is not as easy as it looks. And it's very dangerous because this killer is out for blood, literally."

"Don't worry Uncle Quincy, I'll be careful. I'll get Natalie to help me, she has an intuition for news and murders, anything in the media. I'm sure she would be interested."

"If you both solve this, I can guarantee you great jobs."

"Thanks Uncle Quincy, I'll start on this right away."

Taylor left and Quincy was left to his own thoughts.

"Chances are, nothing will happen. Taylor is a good kid, but he's more the office job type, not the grand master planner and achiever. But hey, people get lucky sometimes and Taylor may get lucky. With Natalie helping him, they might actually discover something."

*****

Mandy was intrigued by the fact the serial killer was actually killing victims according to the zodiac. She was convinced this was a supernatural rite, but she wasn't familiar enough with magic to figure out what could he need twelve victims for. She considered contacting Cornelia Hodgkins. Cornelia Hodgkins is a white witch as well as an astrologer she met at a convention years ago. They connected cause they both lived in the area of Pleasant Falls. She was very well versed in many areas of metaphysics. If anybody could offer insight as to what may be happening, it would be Cornelia. She figured it wouldn't hurt to ring her up and see what she might be able to contribute.

"Hello."

"Hi Cornelia, this Mandy Cummings. We met a while

back at an astrology convention."

"Ah Yes, I remember you. How are you doing these days?

"Well, I still practice astrology and tarot cards, but I still have to learn how to market myself well, so income is sketchy at best."

"I know what you mean, it's hard making a living as an astrologer nowadays. What can I help you with today?"

"Well Cornelia, this is going to be a very unusual question, but I don't if you are aware of the deaths that have been taking place in Pleasant Falls lately.

"Oh yes, it's terrible what's happening over there."

"It's worse than it appears on the surface. These are supernatural motivated murders. The victims are drained of their blood. Each victim is of a different zodiac sign in succession. The last one was a Cancer, I know the next one will be a Leo. The police have transferred them to the hospital and they're not dead, but they're not alive either. I was wondering if perhaps you would know of any ritual magic in which involved offerings of the blood of women, according to astrological signs. Now, this could strengthen the power of the spell or the sorcerer, and the fact that it's blood, is it possible this is ritual designed to either awake demons or create a special situation? "

"Well, to my knowledge right now, no. In the old days, and I mean thousands of years ago, human sacrifice was done for the sake of the crops for if bad weather, like drought, had affected the land. But in this modern age, I have no idea what he is using the blood for. I think this guy is just crazy."

"Yes, I want to believe that too, but it goes beyond that. Somehow, the blood is being drained from these women. Now you would think that would be enough to kill them. But they're not really dead, just in a very strange state. So, whoever is doing this has to have some kind of power."

"That is definitely very strange and very scary. The only thing I can think of is a ritual for personal power. Something in the blood of the twelve women will give the sorcerer whatever kind of power they wouldn't have otherwise."

"However, let's look at a more down to earth explanation. Let's say somehow this person, whether a man or a woman, has developed a way to extract the blood from a body. He could be believing a myth that has nothing to do with the supernatural. For instance, in the 1600s, 1700s, I forget which, there was an ambassador to Vienna from a country in Europe, I think Poland. It was a female ambassador. Somewhere along the line, she learned or was told drinking the blood of young women would keep her young and give her long life.

"So, she would routinely go about having her people round up a young girl, had her killed and then drank her blood. Because of political reasons between Vienna and her country, the authorities looked the other way. There was absolutely no truth to this blood drinking business, but nevertheless, she engaged in this horrible ritual regularly because she thought this myth was real. Who knows how many girls lost their lives to this monster. Nothing ever happened to her. So, there you have an instance where it was simple human debauchery committing crimes.

"Unfortunately, the human race is not very evolved. The dinosaurs lived on earth for hundreds of millions of years. I am willing to wager ten dollars that in all that time, not one dinosaur ever killed another for sport, or out of malice. They killed either to eat or to defend themselves. However, humans regularly kill other humans out of malice, greed, to make their lives easier, out of self-perceived superiority, just about any excuse under the sun. Scientists have said the human race will eventually evolve to level one. However, as you can see, no matter how much time marches forward, we seem to become dumber and more hateful. So, I don't think we'll ever get to level one because we'll probably annihilate ourselves first."

"Well, when you put it that way Cornelia, it's possible we are making too much out of these seemingly "supernatural" connections. Perhaps it is as you say, just plain old murder. And this guy mistakenly thinks that if he kills these women systematically according to the zodiac, something will happen. But that something is all in his head."

"Exactly. One thing I've learned from being involved in magic all these years is before looking for a supernatural solution, just use a normal one. It's a lot easier to tape a piece of paper on the wall than to try to keep it up with levitation. Anyway, that's all I have to add to this situation. I hope this maniac is caught before another woman loses her life."

"Me too Cornelia, me too."

Mandy hung up from Cornelia, and thought about what she said. She's not really back at square one, she just needs to look at this from a different perspective. The inexplicable part of this situation is the drained blood. There's no incision and the bodies are drained. How is that being done she asked herself? She thought maybe this guy does have some weird technology. Something he devised himself. A lot of psychopaths in this world are very intelligent.

Well, back to the drawing board, she thought to herself.

Eleanor Kittering

CHAPTER SEVEN

The next morning, yet another woman is found dead on the street. This was murder victim number five. The Daily Rag carried the story, speculating what serial killer could be doing this and the town had gone into panic mode. Nothing like this had ever happened in Pleasant Falls, and nobody seemed to have a clue as to why it was happening. At this point, Fred called Mandy.

"Mandy, you were right. After we identified the victim, we looked at her date of birth and she is indeed a Leo. The killer is definitely following the pattern you predicted. Meanwhile, that's the only fact we have. Everything else is a mystery. The victim had been drained of her blood, like the others and found with all her belongings. Meanwhile, I'm under a lot of pressure to solve the crime because Quincy is breathing down my neck, he's worried about his re-election. Like this is something I want, some psycho killer running around loose and that's why I haven't solved this problem. Another problem is that Steve Tyrell is really running with this ball and spouting off the dangers of this serial killer, so he's not helping matters."

"So sorry to hear this Fred. We've never had this before and I wonder why are we having this situation now. It's very strange."

"Yep, somewhere in this town there is a killer that is draining women of their blood and I gotta find him before he strikes again. Listen Mandy, I'm going to ask you something that is going to sound very bizarre."

"Sure, anything that might be able to help."

"Can you ask Roger if he has any ideas as to what may be happening? He solved the hedge fund murder, and he knew when those people were coming over your house, the guy intent on killing you and the other woman. So, it's possible he can get an inkling about something that might be eluding us regular people. Perhaps he sees the world differently. You know I'm desperate when I'm asking help from a cat to solve a murder."

"I will definitely let him know what you said Fred. At this point, every little bit helps and who knows, he may figure something out. "

"Ok, thanks a lot. I gotta go, I have Quincy outside wanting an update on what's happening."

"Sure Fred. I'll ask Roger."

Mandy hung up from Fred and started to think at how strange things are going. Her quiet protective cat is now being sought after for criminal advice. And she knew that he could think and could understand human speech. Well, may as well ask him, she thought, and see what kind of a reaction I get.

"Roger honey, are you here? Are you sleeping?"

Roger came out of the other room with Lana.

"No Mandy, Lana and myself were having a discussion. What's up?"

All Mandy could hear was a strange meow.

"Oh good, you're awake, I didn't want to disturb you. You're going to think that this is an unusual request, but there's a serial killer on the loose. Fred is asking your help with any ideas that you may have in catching the criminal. You impressed him in the way you handled the hedge fund case and he needs all the help he can get with this new case."

"Hear that Lana, Fred wants my help. Things must be really bad. I better nod to let Mandy know that I will help."

Mandy heard Roger meowing strangely and nodding. To her, this meant he would help.

"I'm glad that you can help Roger. Is there anything else you want to tell me?" Mandy brought out her tablet.

Roger typed. "Cat small. Nobody notice."

"Yes, that is true, nobody is going to suspect a cat of following them. But don't get too close Roger, this guy is dangerous."

Roger typed again "What crime?"

Mandy upon reading this thought he wanted more info "The information we have so far Roger is that a serial killer out there. Kills women and drains them of their blood. Leaves the body with all their belongings. So far four women have died. People are scared."

"Great. This guy sounds like a psychopath. Give me the tablet again."

Mandy saw that Roger wanted to type on the tablet.

"Anybody see?"

Mandy saw this and said "Nobody has seen him Roger. Only thing so far is they find the body dead the next day drained of its blood. No ransom demands, no demands of any kind."

"Strange. Very strange. What is he doing with all that blood?" he asked rhetorically. All Mandy heard was more strange meows She thought it was frustration.

"I know Roger, it's frustrating because he has covered his tracks very carefully. There's no trace of him and these mystery deaths. That's all. Oh, one more thing, all the bodies wind up in Main Street."

"Wow, this guy has gall. Not only does he kill them, but then he places the body where everybody can see it. And nobody has seen him. Very strange."

"You want to type on the tablet Roger?"

Roger typed "Very strange."

"Another strange thing Roger, he's killing women following the zodiac, so he has seven more women to kill. This will happen in the next two weeks. He's killed five so far, and each following a different sign of the zodiac."

"This gets weirder and weirder. No wonder Fred is asking for help."

"Yes Roger, it's very strange." Mandy couldn't tell what he said, but she figured he was elaborating on his strange reply. Roger motioned for the tablet again.

"I help."

Mandy said "I knew you would sweetie. We'll see what happens."

So, things were left at that. Mandy still couldn't believe that Roger could talk, and that he could communicate his feelings on the matter. Roger on the other hand, went to the next room to think about the situation and talk with Lana.

"This has got to be pretty bad if Fred wants my help. I think I'm going to go tonight and see if I see any suspicious character. Chances are, nothing will happen. That's usually how it is, when you're looking for these dirtbags, they're nowhere to be found. When you're not looking that's when they appear. It's like they have radar of something."

"Well, don't try any heroics." Lana said.

"Look, I'm just going for a reconnaissance trip. See the lay of the land, where the victims are found, that sort of thing. I'm sure I'm not going to see anybody. But if I do, and the victim is still alive, I gotta do something for him to let her go and perhaps she can run away. But chances are, nothing is going to happen."

"Well, be careful."

"I'm always careful."

"No, you're not."

"Great, now I got a mother hen looking after me. Look Lana, I understand you're concerned. But the truth of the matter is that women are dying out there and for no good reason. I gotta do something. The chief of police is at a loss, this cannot be your regular run of the mill criminal. No, he has some kind of agenda. I don't know what it is. But even if all I do is see the guy, it's a leg up. Nobody's seen him as of yet.

"When are you thinking of going."

"I'll probably go after dinner. I'll go to Main Street where he dumps the bodies. It's possible that's where he picks them up too.

Roger waited till it got late. He figured this guy is not going to go out hunting when it's crowded. He's going to wait till it's late and the crowds thin out. But there was still some traffic.

"Well, I'm heading out there, let's see maybe I'll get lucky."

"It all depends on how you define luck. Encountering this guy in the night is not my idea of luck."

"Well, when you're looking for a criminal and nobody knows who it is, that's luck."

"Well, try to get back in one piece."

Roger didn't want to get Mandy involved. Even though according to Mandy this guy is killing by the Zodiac, he didn't want to tempt fate. What's to say that the Zodiac isn't coughing up and he decides to take what's closest. That could be Mandy. No, better he goes alone and see if anything happens or turns up.

It took Roger quite a while to get to Main Street. His little cat legs were not the same as a man's leg that he used to have. Well, eventually he got there. At least he managed to take a walk outside without anybody hassling him. Main Street was still petty crowded in spite of the later hour. And in spite of the killer. That's one thing, no matter how serious things get, people will not be deprived of their good time. And then something goes wrong and everybody gets sad. Roger saw several young women out on the street. Any one of them could be the next victim. He hoped that today wouldn't be a day the killer would go hunting for victims.

Hours went by it got later and later. Roger estimated it was well past midnight. However, this was not the first time in his life that a stakeout turned out to be a bust. He told himself, he'll stick around for another hour and go home after that. Then, he heard it. At first sounded like a whimpering, then he realized that was someone's mouth being muffled, and then a "let go of me". Roger ran in the direction of the sound and sure enough he came upon a guy holding a woman with an armlock around her neck. Roger could see that she was fading fast. The guy was waiting till she became unconscious.

Roger did the only thing that he thought at the time: save the woman by attacking the killer. He started running towards the killer, to get a running start. Cat feet sure are quiet, good for sneaking up on people. He jumped and landed on the guy's back, and moved onto his head. Once on his head he started scratching and biting and yelling "Let her go now!" The guy moved strangely. Even though Roger scratched him hard and blood was oozing down the sides of his face, he didn't flinch much. While Roger attacked his head, he put the woman down on the sidewalk. The voice in side Eli's head told him "Kill the cat". Once she was on the sidewalk, with one hand he pulled Roger off his head and threw him.

Roger said to himself "Man, this guy is strong" while he flew through the air. Roger hoped that he would land somewhere soft. Unfortunately, he hit a tree, full force. Roger saw his vision grow dark. He passed out.

The killer continued with his exercise of getting this woman, she was still unconscious on the sidewalk. Meanwhile, nobody else was around at that time, it was very quiet. He had relieved himself of that annoying cat, like swatting a mosquito. Now he proceeded to carry the woman back to his car. He put her in the trunk and got into the car. Once in the car, in his mind, he started to talk to his lady love.

"Oh my dear, I have yet another woman to offer to you, so that you can soon be free and we can be together. I can't wait to hold you in my arms and kiss you. We were meant to be together and the blood of this woman is one step closer to that reality."

*****

The morning sun came up and Roger still laid in the grassy knoll that surrounded the tree. Perhaps it was the sun's rays, maybe he just regained consciousness but Roger opened his eyes and asked himself, 'what am I doing here?' The he remembered, attacking the killer trying to take him down and the killer throwing him like he was a baseball and the tree he hit was a bat. He was still a little shaken but at least he didn't feel any broken bones. In his mind

Roger thought "There's going to be payback for this buddy, just you wait."

He thought he should go home but then he thought, it's probably better to visit Fred. The police station wasn't that far from where he stood, and he was probably the first entity to ever have an encounter with the killer. Fred would like to know about this. He also realized wearing that ski mask is going to make for hard identification. But at least he knew his height, his build and things of that nature.

Roger arrived at the police station and sat at the desk sergeant's desk. "I want to see Fred." Roger said. All the desk sergeant heard was this very strange meow.

"Hey, is Mandy around? That cat of hers seems to have gotten loose."

"Nope, I haven't seen her. The cat probably went for a walk and came to see Fred."

"Fred? He likes Fred??"

"Seems that way, Mandy brings him over now and then. Maybe the cat has formed an emotional attachment to Fred. I read this in a book about cat feelings."

The sergeant rolled his eyes and shook his head. "Well, Fred is not going to like this, but I don't know what to do with this cat." He rang the intercom for Fred's office.

"Yeah Harry, what's up?"

"Mandy's cat is out here by himself. He walked in and he's sitting on my desk."

"I'll be right out." Fred came out hoping that Roger had something for him.

"Hey there buddy, what brings you around these parts? I'll take him Harry, I'll call Mandy and have her pick him up." Fred took Roger into his office.

"So Roger, you got anything for me."

Roger nodded. Fred took out the tablet so Roger could write.

"Saw and contact killer."

"You saw the killer? You had contact with him? This is amazing. What happened?" Fred cleared the tablet so Roger could write.

"Almost kill me. Hit hard."

"Wow, are you ok now?"

Roger nodded.

"Did you get a good look at him? Can you describe him?" Against Fred made the tablet available to Roger.

"Wear ski mask. Tall. Lean. Very strong."

"So, he's wearing a disguise. Of course. How were you able to get close to him?"

"Nobody suspect cat. Surprise attack."

"And that's when he hit you. Was he angry?" Fred put out the tablet for Roger.

"Not normal. Quiet. Machine."

"So, you're saying he didn't react, he just took you and hurt you."

Roger nodded.

"So we're up against a nut job."

Roger nodded again.

"Well buddy, I gotta tell you, so far you're ahead of everybody in this town. You saw the guy, you tried to take him down, he almost killed you, but at least we learned something."

Roger nodded and asked for the tablet. Fred placed it for him.

"No tell Mandy."

"Oh no, don't worry. If Mandy found out this guy tried to hurt you, she'll never forgive me if something horrible happened to you. No this is going to be our little secret. Roger, I want to thank you for taking this on, originally, I just asked for ideas, I didn't think you were going to go full vigilante on me. I'll say this for you Roger, you got guts. Maybe you're a little nuts too." Fred said laughing.

Roger nodded.

"Ok, c'mon, I'm going to take you home. That way Mandy will think that you came to visit me."

Fred picked up Roger and headed out of the police station.

"Harry, I'll be right back. I'm taking Roger here back to Mandy. I think he likes the police station or me, I can't quite make up my mind." Harry laughed.

CHAPTER EIGHT

Fred got to Mandy's house in no time. He rang the bell. Mandy was asking herself, who would come by this early?

"Fred? Roger?"

"Yeah, apparently he decided he wanted to visit me. He came by the station. Probably needed to take a walk."

"He walked all the way to the police station? That's far."

"Yeah, that's what I thought. Anyway, I thought I would save him the walk back and take him here. Besides, I needed to get out of there. Still no break in the case. And Quincy is still on my back to solve this case."

"What does he think you're going to do?"

"I don't know, he thinks I can magically solve this case. Anyway, I gotta get back to the office.

"Ok Fred, maybe I'll drop by later when I do my groceries."

Mandy took Roger and put him on the floor.

"I see you've taken to it heart when Fred asked you for ideas. Just take care of yourself Roger. I don't want you to become a victim like these other women."

"Don't worry Mandy, I won't be approaching that guy again." All Mandy heard was meows.

During this conversation, Lana walked into the living room. She asked him "How did it go last night.

"I found him alright, but he was a bit stronger than I bargained for. He picked me up and threw me as thought I was a rag doll. I hit a tree and was knocked out."

"Oh Roger! Are you ok? Did you break any bones?"

"Well, no, but it certainly felt at the time like I did. There's something very weird about our perp, normal people don't act the way he was acting. It was as though he was under a trance or something. Usually, these criminal types will show emotion and fight back. I was really tearing into this guy, clawing him, and he didn't even flinch. Not a sound, not an angry retort, no cursing nothing. He grabbed me and threw me, like I was a gnat annoying him. That was the closest I've ever come to flying in my life."

"And then what happened?"

"I passed out. I woke up later and went to Fred's office. He was happy I at least saw the guy. He's very frustrated with this case and not getting any leads. So far, I'm the only one that has gotten a look at this guy."

"What does he look like?"

"You can't tell because he wears a ski mask. But he's tall and thin. And strong."

"Now what happens?"

"Well, after I recover for a day, I'll go back out again and see if I see this guy in action."

"But aren't you afraid he'll hurt you again?"

"Well, this time I'm not going to be foolish and engage him. There's something strange about the guy. This time I'm going to follow him. He was taking the woman to a car so, whatever is going on, is going on somewhere else. He's not doing his blood sucking thing right there and then like a vampire. No, he likes to do his thing in private.

"Obviously, if these women are sucked dry of their blood, there's gotta be a machine or something doing this. He isn't doing this by himself, without the aid of machinery. The human body has a lot of blood, far more than one individual can drink. So, he's extracting the blood somehow and then storing it somewhere for the future. Why, I don't know, but you can be sure it has something do with the supernatural. Probably an idiot who believes in blood sacrifices and other weird things. I don't even know what to speculate on, that would require blood sacrifices for. But it's usually some horrible thing or another."

"I still don't like it."

"Well Lana, so far I'm one of the few entities on this earth that can get close to this guy. I'm a cat, most people don't suspect a cat is keeping tabs on them. So, it's easier for me. And this guy has got to be stopped. Too many innocent lives on the line. This is what happens when you're a cop, you stay on the case until you finally crack it and keep the bad guys off the street. The trick is to do that and stay alive at the same time."

All of a sudden, out of nowhere, there is this strange young woman in the room. She's dressed in garb not really of this century, something from the past, but you couldn't tell the era for certain. She seems to be getting used to these surroundings, as though her regular surroundings are darker than this. At first, Roger thinks this is one of Mandy's friends. But he has never seen this woman before and decides he's going to try to talk to her.

"Hi, can I help you?"

"I was told I could find the great detective Roger Fahey somewhere here."

"I see, what's your name?"

"Lucinda D'Avellaine, daughter of the ruler of Avellaine of southernmost Northchester.

"Lana, are you able to understand this woman?"

"Yes, I can't believe it, I can understand everything she's saying."

"And she was able to understand me. I'm talking with my regular voice."

Lucinda looks at Lana and then Roger and says "Oh, you're cats." As though this was some great revelation to her."

"Yes, we're both cats. This is Lana and I'm Roger. Roger Fahey, as in detective Roger Fahey."

"You're Roger Fahey? But you're a cat!"

"Yes, I know, I get that a lot. How'd you find me?"

"You were recommended by a spirit. I didn't know you were a cat."

"Well, I guess I'm the talk of the spirit world. I gather you're a ghost as well?"

"I think, I'm not sure."

"I see."

"Well, why don't' you tell me what you need me for?"

"Well, I don't truly know what is happening, but whenever I appear, bad things happen to women."

"Are you doing this?"

"No, but I'm somehow associated with it, I don't remember."

"What else can you remember?"

"I'm pretty sure there's a witch involved. I'm usually

walking around in a fog, but whenever I stop drifting, that's when these horrible things start happening."

"Are these horrible things something like mass murders?"

"Yes, a lot of women die whenever she shows up somewhere, but it's not me, it's this witch."

"Well, at least it's not vampires. I believe more in a witch than I do in vampires. The only vampire I know is a guy by the name of Bela Lugosi, and he's not a real vampire, he just plays one in the movie."

"What is a movie?"

"Oh boy, I can see I have a lot of ground work to cover here. How long have you been dead?"

"I don't know, I don't remember. I just seem to float in a fog all the time. I know the witch is the cause of this."

"Can you remember your life before you died?"

"Just bits and pieces. I know I was a princess and somehow this witch is responsible for my death."

"Well, we don't have princesses anymore, unless you count some of the society dames that have an inflated opinion of themselves."

"Oh, but you still have dames."

"Probably not in the way you think."

"Ok, so let me get this straight, you're a ghost, you were killed by this witch, you don't remember when you died, and you drift around most of the time, but whenever you stop drifting, you know this witch is doing horrible things, like she did to you, but she's doing it to dozens of women."

"Yes, that's about it. I wish I could be more helpful, but I don't remember."

"And you say a spirit recommended me?"

"Yes, I was asking for help, because I knew I had stopped drifting and I was mentioning to no one in particular and out of nowhere, this spirit appeared and said "Seek out Roger Fahey, he's a detective, he will help you.""

"So, I'm famous in the spirit world. Who knew?"

"Yes, but you're a cat, now I see this spirit was playing a prank on me."

"Now, now hold on little sister, don't get all upset. I'm not what I appear to be. You see, I had something bad happen to me too. I used to be a man, I was killed by some very bad people and my guardian angel tried to help me to live out the rest of my life, but as a cat. That worked out for a while, but then I had an accident which reminded me I was really a man, so I'm living as a man in the body of a cat."

"So, I was well advised?"

"Yes, you were. It's all very interesting. You see, I am investigating a very strange case in which young women are being found with their blood drained. I saw the man who was doing it. But now that you say there's a witch involved, maybe this guy is a witch."

"No, it was definitely a female witch. That much I remember."

"Well, that may explain something that happened, because when I was attacked by this same guy he seemed to be in a trance. He's the one collecting the females and draining their blood."

"I'm sure the witch has him under a spell. The reason I don't remember my life, may very well be because I'm under a spell the witch put upon me as well. If I remembered why I show up, I could be of more help."

"Well, you have definitely helped so far. At least now we're certain this is a supernatural thing, which explains why the women are drained of their blood and the blood is probably being used for some ritual by the witch. Probably to make her all powerful or something. Humanity has a history of thinking if they drink the blood of young people that youth, eternal life or amazing power will be theirs. There's a lot of sick people out there that will kill for the possibility of this."

"So, you believe me when I say there is a witch?"

"Lucinda, let's put this in its proper perspective. You are a ghost, talking to a cat, who is really a man in a cat's body. At this point, I believe the tooth fairy will come along any time and join us for tea. So yes, I believe there's a witch. Now we have to figure out where she's living and how to stop her. I'm sure she's living in the house of her muscle man, the guy who gets the women for her."

"You have a tooth fairy? Why would you have a fairy for teeth?"

"It's an expression and a long story. We'll focus on the situation at hand and see if we can track down this witch. In the meantime, why don't you spend time with us and maybe you'll remember more?"

"That would be nice. I spend all my time travelling around in a fog alone and I truly don't remember what happened to me or why I always stop drifting when these bad things happen."

"I understand perfectly. Up to very recently, I thought I was a cat and all I had was cat thoughts. Then one day I had an accident and the mechanism my guardian angel had set up broke and now I'm aware I'm a man, I remember everything about my previous life, except now, I'm living in a cat's body. So, it's possible you'll have an experience which will bring back all the memories from the past and you'll finally figure out how this witch is entangled with your life. And maybe finally break that bond. With any luck, if we get the witch, we'll resolve our issue and your issue too."

"Thank you very much. I truly hope I get a solution and answers to my problem, because I truly don't know how long I've been like this."

"Well, if you remember anything else, tell me or Lana here and hopefully that will bring us closer to the truth."

Lana said "Yes, meantime we'll keep you company." Making Lucinda smile.

In the middle of this, Mandy came in the room.

"Roger, you sure are talkative these days. I don't know what you're saying, but if you need anything, you can always to talk to me on the tablet. I don't know what happened to you, but I think you're some kind of phenomenon. So, you're always welcome to talk to me honey."

"Thanks Mandy." All Mandy heard was a strange meow.

"Lucinda, this is Mandy. She is the woman that takes care of us. She got us as pets, and then I had my revelation and since then, she doesn't know what to make of me, but she's very nice and understanding."

"You think I can talk to her?"

"Go ahead and see if she hears you."

"Hi Mandy, my name is Lucinda d'Avellaine." Mandy just kept looking at Roger and Lana, wondering what Roger was saying, but she couldn't hear Lucinda.

"Lucinda, I don't think she can hear you. Not all humans can hear spirits."

"Yes, I've tried in the past and nothing happened. Well at least I can talk to you two."

"Yes, anytime you have something to say, you can share it with us, no matter how unusual it might be."

"I'll keep that in mind."

CHAPTER NINE

Fred was alone in his office. He'd been there since early on since he hadn't been able to sleep. The more he thought about this case, the more he wondered how he was going to solve something that was obviously supernatural. But he didn't believe in such things, so he didn't want to dwell on them too long. The doctors that had lent their support to this case said it was impossible to drain a body of just its blood. And there were no incisions showing how this blood was drained. Men of science were baffled, so what did he have to go on? The only "person" that had seen this guy and actually tried to take him down was a talking cat. A cat! So, maybe he should be more receptive to allowing himself to accept anything is possible and this case so no more innocent people die.

In the middle of his musings his intercom rings.

"Hi Fred, the mayor is out here and he wants to talk to you."

"Great, send him in" Fred thought to himself, this is all

I needed, the most unhelpful person in the world paying me a visit right now. Fred had a pretty good idea as to what Quincy Wells had on his mind.

"Hello Fred, how are you doing this morning?"

"Not too good Quincy, trying to fix this serial killer problem."

"That's precisely why I came to talk to you Fred. Things are looking bad for me Fred, and I don't think you're up to the job for solving this problem."

"Quincy, I'm giving every resource possible to solving this problem, there are volunteers who are looking out to report anything, no matter how trivial, so we can investigate immediately. We've never had anything like in the past and believe me it doesn't make me happy. Innocent people are dying and nobody knows why or how. And that's what I'm trying to fix."

"Fred, I'm sure your heart is in the right place. But my ratings are down more than ever and my opponent is using this opportunity to put me down and say that I'm not doing a good job. Once that kind of talk gets around it may mean the end of me as mayor of Pleasant Falls. All over a crime that isn't being solved quickly enough. I've been mulling calling in the FBI and meanwhile having Taylor to take over the police department."

"Taylor! Are you kidding me? Taylor is a nice kid, but he's never held a job and he has no criminal experience whatsoever. You'd really be shooting yourself in the foot if that happens. If things look bad now, things will go from bad to worse very quickly. Look Quincy, look at the crime rate in Pleasant Falls over the last twenty years. It's always been taken care of. You know why? Because I've been on the job Quincy, because I care for the people in this town, because I know them and they know me and over time people come to me with problems before they hit the papers and before they become a crisis. You can't have that kind of relationship with the people unless you respect them and trust them as well. You throw somebody like Taylor into the mix, whereas before people we're confused and feeling bad about the situation, they're going to lose hope because the one person they trust is out, and an inexperienced person has been put in charge."

"You think that would really happen?"

"Quincy, I'm telling you, if you think your ratings are bad now, putting a completely inexperienced person in this post is going to really erode people's confidence in you and your judgment, no offense. Look, this isn't even a plead for my job, this is a plead for the law and order of this town in a crisis situation. I am not going to abandon these people when they need me and the rest of the police department the most. If you're going to replace me, at least get one of my men who knows what they're doing. But Taylor is going to blow up in your face. Again, nothing against Taylor, he's a good and bright guy, but not the man for this job."

Quincy mulled this over for a couple of minutes, realizing a lot of what Fred is saying is right.

"Ok, I'm going to do this, I'll give you two more weeks to come up with something, otherwise I'm calling the FBI. I can't continue to stand by while my ratings drop and people lose faith in me as a leader."

"Quincy, how do you know your ratings are down? You want my advice? Stop looking at your phone and the social media garbage and go out in the street and talk to the people, listen to what they're feeling, assure them you're doing everything you can to get this situation under control. Those kinds of action re-assure people that Quincy is looking out for them and they start thinking, hey, things are bad but Team Quincy is on the case. Get off your phone Quincy and start looking at real life."

"You may have a point Fred."

"Quincy remember, I'm on your side, you can be the mayor forever. Right now, I need support in this situation, not being thrown to the wolves."

"Ok Fred, but the two weeks still stands. I think the FBI would be an asset here."

"Alright, give me two weeks and let's see where we are then. Hopefully, this will be wrapped up by then."

Quincy left the office and Fred just gave a sigh of relief. He said to himself, I got to get a cup of coffee or something. He waited till Quincy was long gone and he left. As he left, he told the desk Sergeant "Harry, I'm going to the mall to get a coffee. If anybody asks for me, tell them I went to see a man about a horse." Harry smirked, knowing Fred had just met with the mayor and was going crazy.

Meanwhile, Natalie Martin, speculating on what she could do to cover some aspect of this serial murder situation, had come up pretty empty handed. Nobody had an idea, Fred Stone did not want to be interviewed and nobody had an idea how this was happening. The only person to come forth with a theory was Jack Connor the UFO specialist. She was being pressured to put together a show regarding the current situation and this was the only person who was willing to talk. So, she thought, I'll interview this guy, keep it short and listen to what he says on the subject. At least she delivered a show.

"Ladies and gentlemen, thank you for joining us today on this week's episode of "Could it be Real?" where we explore alternative views on life. Today we are interviewing UFOlogist Jack Connor who has some theories regarding the recent murders plaguing our town. Jack, thank you very much for joining us."

"Thank you for having me Natalie. I'm glad you're a forward-thinking person who is not afraid of the truth. Natalie some of the things I'm going to share with you today are going to be disturbing but I am saying them because of my decades of experience as a UFO investigator, with experiential knowledge of aliens."

"Well Jack, we're definitely interested in your thoughts on the matter. Hopefully it may help solve the situation we are in."

"Natalie, this is my honest opinion. These women being killed are being abducted by the aliens. In the seventies, there were cattle mutilations. What happened back then was the aliens would come by in their spaceships and pick up hundreds of specimens of various mammals. I think their main point focus was milk, since milk is such an integral part of human culture.

"Now, I believe that the situation is getting dire for them because they are abducting women.. The main reason they're probably doing this is because they're creating a serum. By extracting a serum from the blood of these women, they can create a sort of vaccine that protects them from diseases that although not harmful to us, would be deadly to them. And then they'll start a full-blown invasion. So, this is just the beginning of the end."

"So, this invasion from aliens is not a matter of if, but when?"

"That's right Natalie. As I outlined in my book, 'I'm not crazy, YOU are' I created a time-line going back to the days of the dinosaurs, showing aliens have been planning this for a long, long time."

"But if they were around at the time of the dinosaurs, why not invade earth back then, why now?"

"Well, in my opinion, what they're really looking for are slaves to do their menial tasks. You see, they're such an advanced civilization, that things like everyday tasks are too mundane and trivial for them. They need a more primitive race, like humans, to actually follow through. So, it's only a matter of time before we start answering to our alien overlords."

"Well, that may be the case, but I don't think the earth is going down without a fight."

"It will be very interesting because, comparatively speaking, our technology is primitive. They may have weapons which are going to make us reconsider before engaging in any long term battle with these aliens.

"So, what do you suggest we do in the meantime?"

"Well, they will be using a subliminal method of subjugation, and these are by sending out a certain frequency in the ultraviolet range humans are susceptible to. One way to stave this off is by wearing a tin foil hat that reflects these vibrations and causes them to return to their sender. I give expert instructions in my book 'I'm not crazy, YOU are' on how to build these hats. Using these techniques, we may be able to get a group of humans who will live in caves and keep the human culture alive. The rest will be immediately be taken over."

"Well Jack, we seem to have run out of time. Thank you so much for coming down and sharing your views on this crisis."

"My pleasure Natalie, thanks for having me."

"That was Jack Connor ladies and gentlemen, stating his views on our ongoing crisis in Pleasant Falls. The video will be up on our website for those who were late for the broadcast. Feel free to comment below the video on the website. Tune in next week to "Could it be Real?" when we interview author Daniel Lazuli on his book Encounters with Yeti and Bigfoot. This is Natalie Martin for WFAB."

The camera stopped rolling and the crew started to disperse. Natalie yelled out "Hey everybody, great job today, thanks for your help. The producer, Tom Ashley came over to Natalie and thanked her for putting on the segment. She asked if Jack Connor was out of the building. He assured her he was.

"Tom, I tell you the truth, it was a strong effort of will not to break out laughing at times. I thought he was a scientific investigator, but he just sounds like a looney. I almost lost it when he started talking about the tinfoil hat, and how shows how to make one in his book. I didn't know he had a book, and especially not with that title."

"Well, I had a brief interview with him prior to this a couple of days ago, and he never mentioned any of this. I believe he's been kicked out of so many tv and radio studios over the years, he doesn't really say much when in the interview phase, but once he gets in front of an audience, he just goes off the deep end. The good news is this is just an opinion, we don't endorse or deny it, we just show the news how a local citizen feels about events affecting the community."

"I'm glad you understand Tom, because I was feeling really uncomfortable the more he went on."

"Just another day in the broadcast business."

Mandy had been watching the whole Jack Connor interview on her tv and thought this was insane. This kind of thing is just going to cause more panic. Why are these people airing interviews with a lunatic like this? Mandy called Fred.

"Oh, Hi Mandy, I hope you're calling to give me good news about anything."

"Well, mostly I was calling to tell you not to watch the latest episode of "Could it be Real?". They were interviewing Jack Connor about the serial murders and he definitely thinks it's an alien invasion."

"That guy is an out of his mind lunatic. Why do they even listen to anything he says? I'm not even going to ask what he said."

"Well, most of it was nonsense and most people will

see the guy is out of his mind. But just a thought in case you decided to watch tv and tune into WFAB."

"Thanks for the head's up. Anyway, let me get back to this mess we're in these days."

"Sorry to hear you're so stressed. You want to go to dinner tonight?"

"I'm afraid I'm not going to be very good company. I just truly need a break in this case."

"Well, let me know if you need anything."

"Thanks Mandy, I will."

Roger and Lana were also having a conversation. Roger was particularly perturbed at Jack Connors's remarks.

"In my day, nobody allowed guy like that to get on the radio. They would just write him off as a crazy person, because that kind of talk just creates problems. I'm going to go out there again and see about this serial killer."

CHAPTER TEN

After seeing the crazy guy talking on tv, Roger decided he should go out again tonight and try a second chance at catching the murder. Now he knew a little bit more about him, he worked with the witch, no doubt, as an unwitting assistant, her slave. As a result he found all the more reason to catch this guy. This time however, he would approach things differently. He wasn't going to engage the guy. He figured the best thing to do was to go to midtown, since that's where he saw him last and seemingly that's where he usually cruised for new women to abduct.

Something told Roger to at least let Lana know of his plans. Otherwise he might go missing in action and nobody will know where he is. Until they find the body, that is. He's heard of too many guys who went on these missions without backup. That's why you have a partner when you're a cop. And you call for backup when the situation gets out of hand.

"Hey Lana, just wanted to share something I'm going to engage in."

"Oh, is this something exciting and dangerous?"

"Well, yes it's exciting, but not the kind of excitement you seek out, like going to the Ferris wheel at the amusement park. And yes, it is dangerous. I just wanted to let you know I'm going to try following the killer tonight, and I figured if I go missing, at least you can tell everybody that I'm missing in action tracking the killer."

"Roger, how am I going to tell them where you are? Write them a note? All they're going to hear is bunch of meows coming from me."

"Well, I think if you meow enough they'll figure out you may know of my whereabouts."

"Yes, I can see it all now, hi everybody, the reason why Roger is not around these days is because he was slaughtered by the serial killer. People hear a series of meows and Mandy will ask 'Lana, do you know where Roger went?' and I will reply, yes Mandy, he went searching for that psychopath. And she'll hear a bunch of meows. Meanwhile, Roger is out there somewhere, in need of help but nobody knows where he went because he just disappeared, same way an elephant goes to die."

"Now I regret saying anything."

"Roger, are you crazy? I have a better idea, we're going to go together on the hunt for this serial killer."

"No, no way, if something happens to you, I'll never forgive myself."

"Nothing is going to happen to me Roger. When you find this guy and get on his tail, I will run out of there, go home and tell Mandy. Eventually she'll figure out you're missing, but now I have somewhere we can go back to as opposed to you leaving now and nobody can tell where you went looking for this guy."

"Ok, that makes sense. You want to try the buddy system."

"Yes, the buddy system Roger. One buddy takes care of the other."

"You have a point. Similar to having a partner when you're a cop."

"Exactly, a partner. So, are we on?"

"Sure, but no heroics."

"Roger, when have you known me to be heroic? When trouble comes, I hide under the bed. No, I'm the buddy that runs to get help. You go and get the bad guy."

"Ok, so we'll do that."

Lana patted herself in the back. She could be pretty persuasive when she wanted.

That night, Roger and Lana set out for the Main Street part of town. This is where the big stores are and the area where everybody goes shopping. You would think with all the traffic this area got, somebody would have seen the killer striking. But no. He probably chose it because it had the greatest traffic. And he could pick and choose the right women for his purposes.

For two cats, this was going to be a long walk. Little feet and short legs aren't the same thing as the long legs of a human. Although it would have been a fifteen minute walk for a person, it would be closer to 30 to 40 minutes for a couple of cats. And then, it would be a chancy situation, without any guarantee the killer would turn up this night. They may go out there for nothing. But Roger felt he had to try. Women kept dying and nobody knew where to find the killer. He'd already seen him and he felt that as long as he didn't engage him, he would be alright.

"Well Lana, this is going to be a long haul for us, so I hope you brought your walking legs."

For a moment she asked herself "Does he think I use different legs for different purposes?" But then it dawned on her this must be one of those human expressions Roger was in the habit of using.

"Yes Roger, I am definitely prepared for walking."

"Ok, so here's the plan. Once we get to the plaza we'll walk around for a little while and if we see any action, I will go in the direction of the killer, and you go in the direction of back home. Don't attempt to follow me or try to help me. Last time, this guy just threw me like a baseball and I was lucky I didn't hit anything too hard. That's not to say I'll get lucky next time. This time, I'm just going to follow him and not engage him. Hopefully I can find out where he lives and then tell Fred."

"Ok Roger, but what if I see him hurting you."

"You run home, you don't interfere. This guy is dangerous and I'm used to getting kicked around, you're more delicate. I don't want anything bad to happen to you. So, no matter what happens, you go home, get Mandy. Mandy will have the common sense to realize there is something wrong and then call Fred. Hopefully, they'll be some kind of a lead that Fred could follow and find the killer."

"Ok, I got it, run home and get Mandy, and hopefully she'll get Fred."

Roger and Lana continued walking. The night was very nice, with a full moon. In his mind Roger thought, great, a full moon, this is just the kind of scenario this psycho would pick to kill his next victim. Lana on the other hand, thought of how she wished Roger and her would do more things like this, going out on a walk together, going to the park together, doing fun things together. But ever since he became a man, Roger has been very preoccupied on how he's going to become a man. Although he spoke with her a lot, he didn't play with her the way he used to when he thought he was a cat. Still, life was better than before when she lived with the FBI agent, Agent Brookdale. Although a nice person, she was never home and never had any time to play with her. She knew that she cared for her, but she was very busy. When she had to move, that's when she gave her to Mandy. Mandy always took time to play with her and to tell her nice things.

"This is nice, going out for a walk with you."

"It's definitely a nice night and you're good company."

"Do you feel better now that you have a "partner"?"

"Well, it's the practical thing to do. If bad things happen, one of us can go for help.'"

Eventually Roger and Lana got to Main Street. In his mind, Roger hoped he hadn't wasted his time, that something would come out of all this.

"We finally got here Roger!"

"Yes. It was a haul, but we got here on our own

transportation and didn't have to depend on Mandy. She is still freaked out that I talk and she's at a loss what to do about it."

"Well, you can't blame her. One day you're just a regular cat on other days you're talking and having conversation via meows is bound to throw her for a loop."

"Yes, I definitely freak her out most of the time. Well, I'm glad that she still cares for me and is not trying to get rid of me. Fred would take me in a jiffy though."

"But, what about us?" Lana asked, slightly hurt to be left alone.

"I'd still come and visit you, it's not like I'm going to forget you."

"But it wouldn't be the same."

"Well, don't worry too much, I don't think Mandy is going to get rid of me anytime soon. I'm the closest thing she has to having a guard dog without having a dog at all. So, she feels safe."

"I feel safe too."

"Well, I'm glad I create an atmosphere of comfort all around." Roger said, kidding with Lana.

They continued walking around for an hour and nothing happened.

"You know Lana, this may turn out to be a bust. One of the most boring things in the world is what's known as a stake out, where you watch a house or area, hoping the perpetrator will do something so you can catch them. People spend hours and hours waiting and looking to see if they catch something. So, it may be one of those nights where nothing happens."

"Well, at least we went on a nice walk."

"Let's head over to the plaza area." By now, most of the stores were closed but there were still people walking around. Not too many, but some. They walked around for a half hour longer. Roger was ready to call it a night. Suddenly, he heard the sound of somebody struggling.

"Let me go, you creep!"

"Lana, I think we got some action." They both went in the direction where they heard the commotion. A half block down, Roger could see the killer subduing a woman. In addition to being strong, he did something that would knock these women unconscious before he took them home. Apparently, that was part of the process, had to keep them as intact as possible before the blood exercise.

The woman continued struggling and he had his arm around her neck. Soon she passed out. He carried her on her shoulder and carried her to the car.

"Ok Lana, this is the part where I follow him and you go home. If I don't come back, you get Mandy to get Fred."

"But how, I don't know people talk."

"You'll find a way, just meow a lot telling them you know where Roger is, she'll get the message."

"Ok Roger, but be careful."

"I will."

Roger continued following the killer at a distance, making sure he didn't have a repeat of last time. He saw Eli get to his car, parked on one of the side streets. Eli opened the trunk and put the woman in. Very chivalrous, Roger thought. But he had to run fast. The only thing Roger thought of was to grab a hold of the back fender. That way he could be a stowaway while he drove his quarry home. Once he found where he lived, he'd go tell Fred and Fred could arrest him.

Eli went to the front of the car and got in. Roger latched himself on the fender. These modern cars were not like the old cars, he thought. There wasn't much of a fender to hold onto. Well, he would make the most of it. The car took off. Of course, it figures he would drive fast, Roger thought. It's possible, Roger thought, that the sooner he got home, the sooner he could drink the blood. Maybe this guy is a vampire, Roger thought. Whoever, whatever he was, he was bad news and evil.

So far Roger had done a good job of holding on, but just barely. If only he would slow down, he told himself.

Eli took the corners very fast. After fifteen minutes of this, on one fast corner, Roger lost his grip. Luckily, he landed on someone's yard. He could see the car off in the distance. Roger had no chance of catching up to him. Now, he thought, came the walk back to Main Street and all the way back home. That ought to be fun, with his little legs. If he was a man, this would be no problem. Well, as the Chinese proverb says, the journey of a thousand miles starts with one step. Roger started taking his steps.

CHAPTER ELEVEN

Early in the morning, Eli dropped off another girl whose blood had been drained. He'd find a place on Main Street to drop them off and then go on his way. He usually put them on the sidewalk or another place where they could be easily found. He had no interest in disguising his crimes, he simply found the victims, got the blood and moved on. He had a certain number he was trying to reach. Then Lucinda would be his.

Lucinda told him if he brought her 12 maidens, each of a different zodiac sign, she would be free of the picture, they would love each other, and she and him would live happily ever after. He was getting closer to getting the maidens Lucinda needed to borrow blood from. He had to satisfy his lady love. She had been trapped in that picture for so long and only the blood of these maidens would free her. And then they could be together. It thrilled him just thinking of her. She and him in love forever. Such a beautiful girl. Yes, the day drew nearer when the two of them would be as one. His business of dropping off another bloodless woman over, Eli went back home.

As daylight broke, Billy Stine got ready for another day of pan handling and plain old begging. He had been homeless now for 10 years and he knew nothing else. It started when he stopped taking an interest in life. He decided to be a drifter. No responsibilities and no hassles. Just being free of the whole rat race. It definitely did get tough at times. But now the heat of summer warmed the air and the weather in the little town worked well for him. He had been sleeping on a couch somebody had thrown out. It hadn't made the garbage yet, it remained in the alleyway where they kept the garbage. A comfortable couch, he couldn't figure out why somebody threw it out. But hey, it worked for him, so he was glad someone threw it out. They kept it in that alleyway and he would go there as much as possible.

One thing about being a homeless person is you always have to keep moving. You don't want to be found by anybody cause otherwise they think you're an undesirable. As he got to Main Street that morning, he notices the body of a woman across the street. He looks at her and she looks young and pale. Billy thinks this is probably a college student. Too much to drink last night and she passed out on the street. Kids will be kids, always love to party. He remembered when he was young. He wasn't very popular at school. Come to think about it, he wasn't very popular at all. But yeah, he sure liked to drink. When he drank all those bad feelings went away. Those terrible feelings he had of himself, just floated away on a cloud. So, that's probably what happened to this girl. Too much drinking and passing on the street. She must have passed out right there on the sidewalk.

Billy kept walking away but then, he got an idea. Why doesn't he take $5 dollars from her purse? She's young, she probably has a job or a family that's taking care of her. Five dollars wouldn't mean anything. She probably spends that much on coffee at a pop. He thought of how much time he could save pan handling that morning. Those five dollars made the difference of eating now or eating much later, when he could scrounge up enough cash to buy something at the store. He continued walking away but the lure of those five dollars was strong. An easy five dollars. She'll never miss it and when she gets up, she's going to have more important things to think about like, what happened last night.

So, Billy went back and decided to "borrow" five dollars from the girl. When he got up to her, he realized she was paler than most. He didn't want to think about it too much, just grab the five dollars and split. So, he bent over her, looking for her purse. There it was, he opened it and lo and behold, right there, on the top were five dollars. They were singles, but it didn't matter. Easy, peasy process. He put the five dollars in his pocket and started to put the handbag on the side of the girl. Right at that moment her heard a cop say "Step away from the body, put your hands up where we can see them."

Great. Billy thought, the cops. Oh no, they're going to think I rolled this girl. I should have walked away I should have tried to make the five dollars the slow way. The cops approached Billy.

"Officers, honest I don't know what happened to this girl. I just wanted to borrow five dollars for coffee."

The continued cuffing him and reading him his Miranda rights. One of the officers called Fred "Fred, I think we may have a suspect. We found him stooping over the body of one of the women. He says he's trying to borrow five dollars. We're calling the ambulance for the girl."

"Is she dead?"

"Yeah Fred, she's dead just like the others."

"Ok, I'll be right down there."

Fred took off out of the station like a bat out of hell. He asked himself, Could this finally be the killer, could this nightmare finally be over? Well, he'll soon find out.

Fred parked his car near the other patrol car. He walked over to the other two officers.

"So, this the guy?"

"Officer I swear I didn't hurt this girl, I was borrowing five dollars to get coffee, I thought she was drunk and unconscious and I only took five dollars. It would have helped me this morning in getting breakfast."

"What's your name?"

"Billy Stine officer."

"Well Billy, you're in a lot of trouble. We don't know if you hurt this girl or not so we're taking you down to the station."

"I swear officer, I swear I didn't hurt this girl in anyway. She was just laying there quiet with all her stuff as you can see. I thought she had passed out from too much drinking."

"You see somebody on the street who is helpless and instead of helping them, you try to help yourself to five dollars. That's pretty parasitic Billy. You would have taken the five dollars and left the girl there. What if she needed hospital care what if she could be saved? All you could think of was getting five dollars. Well, Billy for your information, the girl is dead and now you're our number one suspect."

"I swear I didn't kill her, you gotta believe me, I just wanted to borrow five dollars."

In the middle of this Quincy Wells arrives in his car.

"Well, well, well, I see you finally caught the killer good work Fred."

Fred asks "Who called him."

"Nobody called me Fred, I've been listening to radio communications to see if any progress is being made."

Quincy walks to Billy.

"So, this is the monster who's been terrorizing the whole town, killing innocent women and draining them of their blood. He doesn't look like much, but these serial killers never do."

"Serial killer! Now wait a second. I've never killed anybody in my life. I just tried to borrow five dollars from this girl. I didn't know she was dead. I thought she had passed out from too much drink."

"A likely story. I better call a press conference so I can inform the people of this town Quincy Wells is on the case and we've caught the killer, the streets are safe again."

Fred heard what Quincy was saying and knew that a media circus would descend on this town. Although he wanted to get the killer as much as anybody, this guy didn't fit the profile of a killer, let alone a serial killer. He was beginning to realize that things were exactly as Billy said. He's homeless, sees an easy five bucks and decided to rob the girl. He walked over to Quincy.

"Quincy, can I talk to your for a minute."

Sure Fred. Don't worry I don't plan to take all the glory. You caught the killer, you will be part of the killer's capture. I want the townsfolk to know what a great police captain we have."

"Quincy, I strongly suggest you don't call any kind of press conference."

"No press conference!? Fred, this is my chance for my ratings to zoom, the townspeople learning the serial killer has been caught. And you're telling me not to call a press conference? No, we have to do this right now."

"Listen to me Quincy, you're making a big mistake. It's still very premature to think that this guy is the killer. Yes, we found him over the body and yes he took money from the woman. But that's it, he doesn't fit the profile. The serial killer is after blood and then dumps the body on the sidewalk. Every single woman we found as victim of this psychopath always has her belongings, money included. This guy here, he wanted five dollars. He's robbing her money.

"Furthermore, if you jump the gun now and we find out he's not the killer, you're going to look like a jackass and your opponents are going to accuse you of setting up a fake capture to get the attention and the votes. It will be far worse than not saying anything. They'll have a field day with you."

"But Fred, he was found over the body, he's gotta be the killer."

"Not necessarily Quincy. He looks to me like a homeless guy. The killer has a very sophisticated setup to extract the blood of these girls. This guy is a clueless homeless man who doesn't have enough sense to not rob from a corpse."

"Perhaps you're right Fred. It's just that I thought it was so exciting the killer was caught while I was still mayor. It would strengthen my position."

"Quincy, I want to get this killer just as bad as you do, but we have to go through the due process of the law. Right now, we're going got take him downtown, and we'll observe him. If he turns out to be the killer, hey, you take the glory, hopefully it will help you get elected. But let's find out for sure first, otherwise, things are going to get pretty ugly if you announce this and then it turns out not to be the killer we're looking for."

"Yeah, you're right Fred. But you call me the moment you find out anything."

"Well, no news is good news. If you don't hear from me, that means this guy is not the killer."

"Ok, I'll be at city hall."

Quincy drove away in his car and Fred heaved a sigh of relief. During this exchange, the ambulance had arrived and was in the process of taking the woman to the hospital. Billy was terrified of his prospects. He just wanted to take five dollars, something nobody would have missed and now he was an accused murderer. He really didn't want to go to jail for a crime he didn't commit. Fred came back to the officers.

"Great, so the woman is on the way to the hospital. Let's go downtown and book this guy. For now attempted murder and we'll see what happens."

"Don't put me down for that, I'm innocent, just a homeless guy trying to get some breakfast money."

Meanwhile back at Mandy's house, Roger had his own certain set of dilemmas. He now had to tell Fred there was a witch involved and this explains the supernatural stuff. This was going to be a tough sell to someone like Fred. But hey, the women are showing up with no blood in their veins. This is not the kind of thing that happens every day. So, if he wants to get the killer, he better start believing in the supernatural. He wanted to go to the police station, but as a cat, it would take him a long time to walk down there. No, he had to get Mandy to give him a ride downtown so he could talk to Fred.

He started meowing at Mandy saying "Mandy, we have to pay Fred a visit, there's something I have to tell him."

Mandy learned when Roger meowed like this, he wanted to tell her something.

"Hi baby. You want to write something on the tablet?"

Roger nodded.

"Ok, let me get it and let's see what you have to say."

Roger typed "Visit Fred."

Mandy read what Roger had typed. "You want to pay a visit to Fred? He may be busy during the day."

Roger motioned to type on the tablet again. Mandy cleared the tablet so Roger could type again.

"Must tell something."

"You want to go visit Fred so you can tell him something?" Roger nodded.

"Is this something regarding the murders?"

Roger nodded again.

"Roger, I don't know how you get this information or how you talk but by now I've learned when you want to talk to Fred, it's something important."

Mandy called Fred. Fred picked up agitated.

"Hi Fred, I hope I'm not bothering you."

"No, you're never a bother Mandy. We caught a homeless guy who may or may not be the killer, we'll know later when we perform lab tests on his prints."

"Ok. The reason I'm calling is Roger wants to talk to you."

"Talk to me? About what?"

"He said it was about the murders."

"Ok, bring him over."

"Well Roger, Fred says to bring you over. So hopefully your information will help catch the killer."

Mandy was very confused about the new Roger. She had a cat who was conscious and able to communicate with humans. And unbeknownst to her, he was investigating this murder. What happened to her old Roger? Mandy remembered the hedge fund situation where Roger knew when the murderer was coming over. He got Fred involved. He didn't try to be a hero. He knew he needed help. Mandy was sure he was doing the same thing. Could Roger be the one to solve the serial killer murders? How was he doing this she asked? On the other hand, how many people can say their cat talks and can understand people. No one. Not like this. Not like Roger. She thought of this while getting ready to leave.

"Lana, we're going to go visit Fred, I think it's better if you stayed, things are always chaotic at the police station. When we come back, we'll do something fun - like go to the park."

Roger translated. "What she's saying is we're going to the police station. That place is full of trouble and is no fun, so you're going to have to stay by yourself. However, when we come back, we may go to the park."

"Great, I feel like a fifth wheel again."

"It's nothing personal Lana, we're trying to solve this murder. You saw that guy. This is not a fun situation and sooner we catch this guy, the sooner peace can reign in the land again."

"Ok. But come back soon."

"We'll get back as quickly as possible. Believe me, I'm not crazy about this whole situation, but I'm the only one that has any information for Fred."

Mandy said "I guess Lana doesn't understand me and you try to explain things to her. That's amazing."

Roger nodded.

It didn't take long for Mandy to reach the police station. She parked and went to the desk sergeant.

"Hi, we're here to see Fred."

"We?"

Mandy picked Roger up "Yes, we."

"Oh, him again." The sergeant pressed the intercom. "Fred, Mandy is here with her cat."

"Send them in."

"Sorry Fred, he really wanted to come see you."

"It's ok Mandy, so far, Roger's the only one that has

good info. Whaddaya have for me buddy?"

Fred put out the tablet for Roger to type.

"Follow killer back of car."

"You tracked him all the way to his house?"

Roger typed. "Fell off car."

"So, you lost him."

Roger nodded. Asked for more typing. Fred cleared the tablet.

"Accomplice. Witch."

"You're telling me he has an accomplice who's a witch."

Roger nodded and asked to type again.

"Witch brains. Man muscle."

"So you're saying there's a witch involved, she's the brains of the outfit, this guy just collects the girls, she does the supernatural stuff."

Roger nodded. He asked to type again.

"Crazy. But true."

"Roger, where are you getting your information from? Can I speak to them, him, her?

Roger shook his no.

"Are you trying to protect your sources?"

Roger shook his head again.

"Am I capable of speaking to this source."

Roger shook his head and asked to type.

"Ghost."

"You're getting your information from a ghost."

Roger nodded and motioned to type.

"Bad supernatural stuff."

"This is just Jim Dandy. I got a case in which a witch is behind the crimes and the main source of this information is a ghost. No wonder I can't get a break in this case. The closest I've come is finding some guy with the body another woman this morning, robbing her. Hey, that gives me an idea. Roger, could you identify this guy if you saw him?"

Roger nodded.

"Great! C'mon buddy, we're going to identify a perp."

"Now, you're talking my kind of lingo." Roger meowed.

"I'm going to take that meow meaning you like this."

Roger nodded.

Mandy felt a little concerned. "Fred, is he going to be ok?"

"Mandy, this is the cat that has saved you from would be murderers. This is the cat that solved the hedge fund case. This is one tough cat. He may be a cat, but he ain't no pussy."

"Listen, I'm going to show you this guy, just nod if yes, shake your head if no."

Fred carried Roger to the holding pen. The other cops were ribbing him.

"Hey Fred, did you get a new pet? You're training him to be a cop?"

Fred just looked at the guys "Everybody's a comedian Roger."

Roger nodded and said "It's the same thing in my time." All Fred heard was meows.

"I gather you understand. Anyway, we're getting close to this guy's cell."

Fred and Roger got to the cell where they were keeping Billy.

"Billy, I came to visit you, to see if your conscience has caused you to tell the truth."

"Did you come to show me your cat as well?"

"Don't get cute Billy. You're in a lot of trouble."

"Look officer, everything I said was true. In retrospect, it wasn't my best judgment to steal from a person I thought was unconscious, but I truly just wanted to get five dollars for coffee. Nothing more, nothing less. I thought she was drunk and had passed out on the street. I didn't know she was dead."

"Billy you try to help people when they're down, not steal from them. Look at this cat. He doesn't approve of your actions. Roger, what do you think."

Roger shook his head, meaning to say this wasn't the guy.

"So, that's it, you come down here to scold me and show me your cat?"

"Billy, don't get uppity. This cat may have just saved your bacon."

"I really just wanted to take five dollars."

"Tell it to your lawyer."

Fred walked away from the holding pen.

"So, was he the guy?"

Roger shook his head.

"What a low life, stealing from a woman out lying on the street. So what if she was drunk. You don't go and steal from her. These guys just lose all sense of ethics."

"Same thing in my time Fred, things haven't really changed."

"I'm going to take that to mean, you disapprove of this guy."

Roger nodded. No use wasting time trying to translate.

CHAPTER TWELVE

The next morning, Roger, Lana and Lucinda were hanging around. Lana was a little concerned about Lucinda.

"You know, I'm a little worried about Lucinda. She doesn't seem too well and rarely if ever talks. I think she feels really bad not knowing who she is and why these women are dying."

"Yeah, she definitely has a problem not remembering what really happened. She feels bad that whenever she shows up, bad things happen, but that's all she has to go on."

"I don't think she has a family either. I think she's all alone in this world."

"Well, it's possible Colin will be able to help her. He's good like that. And she's a spirit, so she's part of the way to where ever she's headed spiritually."

"Hey, that's a good idea, get Colin involved."

"I've been trying to give the guy a break because I'm always dragging him into these messes he has nothing to do with. But this is way beyond me. Some girl who's a ghost and can't remember her past. And bad things happen whenever she shows up. Something is happening here that's not adding up. Fred says he's never been up against anything like this. Neither have I. I only had one experience with a ghost a long time ago. And it wasn't a criminal case."

"Wow, you had an experience with a ghost before? What happened?"

"It was a big disappointment. I don't even like to remember it."

Lana saw this made Roger sad. She thought it better to focus on Lucinda.

"Well, one thing I've noticed Roger is when you put your mind to something, you usually figure it out. I'm sure you'll solve this case and help Lucinda as well."

"Thanks for your confidence in me. I wish I felt that confident myself. But all I do is throw stuff up against the wall and see what works. Sometimes things work, other times, it's back to the drawing board. So far, I've gotten lucky in this investigation.

I still can't figure out why Lucinda came to me. Somebody suggested me as a detective. Am I famous in the spirit world as a detective? Maybe news travels fast that the spirit of a man is inside of a cat, and he's a detective. But I'm not a miracle worker. All I have is that there's some psycho out there getting girls for this witch. She takes their blood. Other than that, I have nothing. Why does she take their blood? Why twelve women? Why here?"

While Roger mused on what was wrong with this case, Lucinda came running into the room.

"I remember! I remember everything! Where am I?

Who are you?"

"This from the one that remembers everything. Lucinda, it's me Roger, remember. I'm the detective, you came to me for help in solving your witch problem.?"

"You're a detective? But you're a cat!"

"Here we go again. Yes, Lucinda, although I appear to be a cat, I'm really a man in a cat's body. I'm a detective."

"Oh, has a wicked witch put a spell and turned you into a cat, a spell that can only be broken with the kiss of a fair princess. I am the fairest maiden in the land and I am also the princess of Avellaine. I am sure a kiss from me will release you from this wicked spell."

"I am touched by your self-effacing modesty, but I don't' think it works that way. This is actually the handywork of my guardian angel gone haywire. I was supposed to live my life as a cat, but then, due to an accident, I remembered that I'm a man. Now I'm a man in a cat's body. But I will keep the kiss from a princess option in mind. At this point, I'm ready to try anything."

"A fair princess." Lucinda reminded Roger. Roger rolled his eyes and whispered to Lana "I think I liked her better when she didn't remember." Lana just said "Shhhhhhhhh."

"Why don't you tell us what you remember, since your recent memories of us seemed to have been wiped out with your remembrance of everything from the past?"

At this moment, Colin appears, and he asks "Roger, you summoned me, I've been trying to deal with your problem, sorry I wasn't able to come sooner."

"No, you're just in time, I want you to meet Modest Michelle."

"Oh noble little cat, you must have misheard. I am Lucinda D'Avellaine, princess of the kingdom of southernmost Northchester."

"You can call me Roger."

Lucinda pranced around happily now that she remembered her previous life. Roger looked at Colin and said "I don't know what's wrong with this one." Colin drew Roger aside

"Roger you have to take it easy on her. She's a lost soul.

"You can tell with just with one look? Boy, you're good."

"I'm an angel Roger. I'm in the spirit business, as you would say. Anyway, let's hear her story. Sometimes these people have been drifting around for a long time."

"So Ms. D'Avellaine, could you please tell us about yourself, for my sake mostly." Colin said.

Well, I am Lucinda D'Avellaine, princess of the kingdom of southernmost Northchester. I was considered the fairest maiden in the land. My best friend and love of my life was Tranthen de Guillaume, the only son and prince of the adjoining Gloustershire. He and I had played since we were young and over time we fell in love. We made up a song we would sing to each other. He would sing:

My precious princess fair
Did pledge her love to me
Her beauty and her majesty
Do cast their spell on me
When winter doth arrive
Her love doth keep me warm
I love her more than life
I pray she'll be my wife

While I then would reply with my chorus:

My precious love and prince
So tender and so warm
You treat me like your queen

So gallant is your form
The Kings may come and go
The world will make amends
The love I have for you my friend
Will never, ever end

"We were so happy and everyone was convinced one day we would wed. Our parents certainly had no objection and welcomed the union. However, my parents would not allow me to marry till I reached twenty one years of age because of a family custom. I had wanted to marry Tranthen since I was twelve, but since we spent so much time together, it really didn't matter.

"One day, I came across this old, disfigured woman. The woman started to yell at me, and telling me to get out of her way. I asked her why she should be so cross with me, I did nothing wrong. The old woman said she was a witch and she didn't like the fact I was happy. Can you believe it? I thought she was a crazy old woman and I laughed at this and said I did not believe she was a witch and be off with her. So the witch put a curse on me that I would die on my 21st birthday and become a lost soul, forever wandering this world. I did not take this very seriously, since I thought she was a crazy old woman.

"Before my 21st birthday was going to be celebrated, my family ordered a portrait be painted of me. It was a beautiful painting, and everyone thought it portrayed a beautiful girl at the height of her beauty. However, at the stroke of midnight on my birthday, I died, without any illness.

"Everybody was incredulous of my death, and my husband to be Tranthen was inconsolable. We were to be wed 2 months after my birthday, when Tranthen would turn 25. I got reports of my previous life in the spirit world, and learned Tranthen was heartbroken and he never did marry anyone else, since I was the love of his life.

"The witch who hated anything beautiful went one step further. She put a spell on the painting that whenever the right sort of man gazed at the painting, he became enamored of Lucinda in the painting. Then, as part of the spell, the man would be hypnotized into thinking if he offered the blood of 12 young maidens to the picture with each maiden of a different astrological sign, I would be brought back from the dead and live happily ever after in love with the man who set me free.

"This was just a ruse invented by the witch to enslave the men with a spell. What the witch was really doing was absorbing the blood of the young women so she could continue living on this earth and maintaining the look of a youthful maiden. And then she'd kill off the men who did her dirty work.

"This has been going on for a long time. The painting has been sold, stolen and sought after in the belief of the legend that if enough young maiden's blood is offered they would get me as a gift for their work. This has never happened and the few men that even mildly engaged in this, when they realized what they were doing, went crazy afterwards and eventually were found dead. I'm always drawn to the painting when it has a new owner, and that's when I appear in one location. That's why I know the painting is in this hamlet.

"I was advised to look for Roger to help me stop the witch from murdering new innocent young women. I knew something horrible was happening every time I made a stop and for years I have not been able to remember. That's why I was so excited when I remembered. I knew why I was here and I had someone to help me stop the witch."

Roger and Colin looked at each other.

"When did this originally happened, when you first met the witch?" Colin asked.

"The year was 1273. What year is this?"

"2019, you've been drifting for 700 plus years."

"700 years! I never knew. It always seems like it happened yesterday, or I don't remember at all."

Lucinda held her hand to her mouth and you could see despair taking over her. Seven Hundred years. She asked herself why did no one ever come to find me? Has everyone forgotten me? What about Tranthen? Is it possible he met another lady fair and forgot about me, she told herself. I've been in a fog for seven hundred years. I can scarcely believe it, she told herself.

Colin saw the realization of time past had hit Lucinda hard. He told her "I will do what I can to help you Lucinda, so you don't have to continue wandering the spirit world in a fog, with no memory of anything."

Roger could see she was almost in tears "Don't worry Lucinda, one way or another, we'll help you. Now we have some real facts and it explains why all these women are showing up with no blood in them. The witch is draining them dry. One way or another we'll find her and put an end to this horrible situation. This may be the last time the witch gets a chance to re-energize herself."

"Thank you both. At present, I am a little overcome at the news that I have been in a fog for seven hundred years. It always seemed like just a couple of days. Maybe someday I'll meet my family again."

Eleanor Kittering

CHAPTER THIRTEEN

Roger and Colin strategized the best way to catch the killer that night.

"I think if we're going to catch this guy, our best bet is to go to the Main Street area. That's where he likes to get his victims because there's a lot of people traffic and he can find the next victim easily. He usually likes to keep the late hours. I'm amazed with all that's going on, there are still young women going out at those times for recreational purposes."

"They don't think it's going to happen to them."

"That's usually the way it is. Well, let's get going, I like travelling with you better. When I'm alone and going on my own steam, these are far distances for a cat to walk. These are the times when I miss not being a man. The mobility is somewhat limited."

"Yes, little feet and small strides don't help in covering long distances."

"You got that right. Another thing I was thinking about is we have to follow this guy tonight once he does find a girl. So, unfortunately, she's going to get knocked out by this guy. However, I'm sure the blood sucking takes place wherever he lives, so we'll prevent that one way or another. Stealth mode is best. Hopefully, we'll be able to follow better than I did, where I fell off the car."

"Don't worry, I have a great technique for following."

"I knew you'd come up with something to make our lives easier. "

Roger and Colin arrived at Main Street at approximately 11PM. It was pretty quiet, but people were still moving to and fro.

"We'll just stake out the place until we hear something. That's how I found him in the past."

Roger hid behind a small extension to a wall and since Colin was an angel, nobody could see him, so as far as the world was concerned, it was an empty street. After 40 minutes of hanging out and making chit chat, they hear sounds in the distance.

"Let go of me, get away from me you creep!"

The killer applied a chokehold until the woman passed out. Then he carried her like a sack of potatoes in the direction.

"Hear that Colin, the killer is striking again. Let's go."

They ran up the block and by the time they made it there, Eli was crossing the street. Roger knew he was heading to his car.

"Let's follow quietly, he usually puts the victims in the trunk of his car. Except this time we're going to follow and see where he lives. Ten dollars says the witch is living there too. "

"I'm sure you're right Roger."

Roger and Colin caught up and easily followed twenty feet behind with the killer unaware they were there. He stopped when he got to this car and started to open the trunk.

"See, this is his whole routine. Knock them out and put them in the trunk of the car. I'm sure the witch puts him in a trance."

Eli got in the car and was ready to drive away.

"Come on Colin, he's gonna get away."

"Don't worry Roger, I got this."

Roger found himself floating off the ground and gliding. Colin was gliding right next to him.

"Hey, this is pretty good. Any way I can get to do this when you're not around."

"Unfortunately not Roger, I am actually doing the heavy lifting. Not that you're that heavy, but I was just using a metaphor to illustrate my point."

"Oh well. I was just hoping. Besides, a flying cat would definitely create a ruckus sooner or later."

"No truer words were spoken."

To Roger, this route looked familiar. He thought, the killer must be a creature of habit. Roger recognized the lawn of the house where he fell off last time.

"This is where I fell last time."

"Well, this time we won't lose him."

Roger and Colin continued following the car, the killer being completely unaware he was being followed. After two miles, they saw an old house up ahead. The killer started to slow own.

"I think we're getting to the lair of doom."

The killer drove into the driveway of a house.

"That's where the action takes place."

After parking the car, the killer got out of the car and opened the trunk. The woman was still unconscious, he put her over his shoulder and started to walk into the house.

"Ok, let's move in so they don't do any harm to the her."

Roger and Colin went to the back of the house. Colin opened the door without any problems. They quietly moved to the room right outside the room where the lights were on. Roger saw a woman, who he assumed was the witch and the guy who had attacked the woman. The witch appeared to be a short middle-aged woman, with dark brown greying hair. She was dressed in modern clothes, but there was something very strange about her. Eli looked like he was still in a trance. There was a long table to the side of the room. Eli put the woman on top of the table. The was a fireplace the opposite side of the room with a live fire going on. On the wall at a right angle to the fireplace, was Lucinda's picture. The picture is what drew these men into the situation in the first place. Lucinda was right. The witch started talking to the guy.

"Great, you've brought me another one. That makes six so far. I am half way to my goal. Very soon I'll have the blood and life essence of all twelve and get a new lease on my life. And I shall look young and beautiful."

Eli stood there with a glassy look in his eyes. Roger thought to himself 'this guy is completely under the witch's control. He's probably not even aware of his actions. He just does what she tells him because he's under whatever spell she put on him.' The witch spoke again.

"No use wasting time. I want her blood and her essence. I love getting this inside me."

The witch started incantations as she waved her hands in the air. Roger said, ok it's time for an intervention.

"I hate to break up this party witch, but there will be no blood for you today."

The witch was startled by this sound, when she thought she was alone.

"A cat! How did you get in here cat? How dare you interrupt me!"

"Oh, I'm here to more than interrupt you, I'm here to put a stop to you forever. You should have died a long, long time ago. But you're still here by killing these women. You steal their lives so you can continue living your evil life. You're nothing but parasitic scum."

"How dare you speak that way to me!" The witch decided to throw a spell at Roger. She raised one hand and sent a bolt of energy at Roger. Nothing happened. The witch was very perplexed.

"What are you cat?"

"I'm your worst nightmare, this is the end of the line witch."

With that, Roger took a run and leapt up at her head. He started to scratch her head and bit her face.

"Get off me you mangy cat. Why isn't my magic working on you."

"Maybe your magic just stinks."

Roger continued to attack the witch. She was strong and pulled on him with all her might. He was beginning to lose his grip, and at one point, one of his paws got loose from her head. In trying to get a grip again, he latched onto her necklace, a big necklace full of large stones. His other paw came loose and now both paws were wrapped around her necklace. The witch continued to pull hard and Roger continued to hold onto the necklace. He felt the necklace coming loose. The witch started to spin around and pull on Roger.

"I'll get you off me cat, and you'll pay with your life."

"Not if I get you first witch. I'm pretty strong."

At one point the witch did a really strong tug pulled the necklace super hard and broke it. Roger went flying to other side of the room. The necklace went flying into the fire. It burst into flames right away.

"My amulet, my amulet!" the witch was screaming, running towards the fire place. Roger seeing that this amulet was probably an important part of her rituals, jumped on her again.

"Oh no you don't. We're going to let that amulet burn to a crisp."

"Get off me cat, you don't understand what you're doing."

Roger continued to bite and scratch the witch's head and she wasn't able get her off him. In the middle of this, the picture started to smoke and parts of it were catching fire. The witch continued screaming.

"No! No! Look what you're doing."

"I'm not doing anything witch except trying to kill you. You never know, I may get lucky."

All of a sudden Lucinda's picture burst into flames. There was a connection between the amulet and the picture. A black arm with leathery skin and claws started to come out of the picture. This was followed by the rest of the body. A horrible looking creature crawled out of the picture, it looked like a giant kangaroo, ten feet tall, with sharp spikes on the end of its tail. It had long claws on its short arms and long teeth all around its mouth, making it look as though it was in a constant perpetual horrific smile. It was a demon. This was what possessed Eli and told him what to do.

"WITCH!!"

Roger jumped off the witch and went to a corner of the room, figuring she had bigger fish to fry now, and he didn't want to get to meet smiling jack from the picture.

The witch yelled to Eli, still in a spell, "Attack the demon". Eli did as he was told and started to charge the demon. The demon simply did a slicing motion and put his claws right through him, killing him on the spot.

"Witch, you tricked me and locked me in that picture so I could do your dirty work for you."

"Oh, that was an accident."

"An accident. Seems like you deliberately set up that amulet to jail me in that picture so I could hypnotize your minions over the years. It's been over seven hundred years witch, I don't think that was an accident."

"Has it been that long? I just lost track of time."

Roger saw that as the witch and the demon were having this discussion, the witch was quietly retreating so she could escape the room and run.

"Why don't you come closer to me witch?"

"Well, after all this time, you probably want some space."

She was almost out of the room, when Roger took a running leap, pushed the witch from behind and sent her into the demon.

"Here Smiley, you can have her with my compliments."

The witch stumbled and tripped into the demon.

"Get away from me demon."

"No witch, you're going to pay with your life."

With that, the demon started to attack the witch with his sharp claws. He stabbed her a couple of times and a strange thing started to happen. Immense quantities blood and light started to come out of the mouth of the witch and shoot out of her like a fountain. As these living materials went up into the air, they escaped the room. After a while, the fountain like effect stopped. The demon continued to attack the witch and the witch tried to defend herself with spells.

"Your magic won't work on me now witch, you're too weak."

The demon was enraged and happy the witch was getting weaker and weaker started killing her with his claws. This created another strange effect. As the demon attacked the witch, she got older and older. Then, at one point, the witch simply started to turn to dust. She was so old, and she had maintained her life artificially that now that someone was killing her, she just disintegrated. The demon seemed pleased with his handywork, but you couldn't tell cause his face constantly showed all those teeth. Roger had been watching the whole proceedings and now that it was over, him and demon locked eyes. The demon did a short nod, and then proceeded to leave by breaking out through the window. Roger heaved a sigh of relief.

"I thought I was a goner there for a moment. I guess even demons have some kind of code -Don't kill the cat that liberated you from a picture and gave you your enemy on a silver platter."

"Yes, I think he was so happy to be free, he didn't want to stick around."

"I could have sworn that at the end there he nodded at me."

"He was acknowledging your help. That's as close to a thank you you're going to get from a demon."

"Colin, a little help would have been appreciated when I was tangling with the witch."

"You had it under control. Besides, I spell warded you, that witch couldn't hurt you with her magic. It was all about the muscle and I knew you would break the amulet."

"You knew about that."

"Yes, and I also knew that you would enjoy taking her down by yourself. You just needed a little help."

"You're right, I enjoyed beating on her. Let's check on the girl, she seems to still be unconscious."

"Yes, she's still under the spell from the demon. The demon possessed the guy and gave him the ability to put a spell on them to make them unconscious, so he could bring them home unharmed, she wanted their blood and their life energy intact. He also gave him incredible strength. The demon did what the witch wanted because he was under a spell from the amulet."

"Yeah, I'm aware about the guy's strength, he threw me like I was a baseball, and I felt like I was flying. It's a shame about the guy though. He really was innocent, he was just a slave for the witch."

"Yes, he's an unfortunate casualty of this whole affair. However, there might be a silver lining to this whole case, but I'm not 100% sure yet."

"Well, I think we should focus right now on saving this one woman and getting Fred to take over. He'll be glad to have solved this crime. And unfortunately, the guy is going to have to be the killer, even though he was innocent. So, hopefully you can help me get to Fred's office quickly."

"Oh, we can get there in no time."

Roger and Colin wound up at the police station. It was about two in the morning. Fred hadn't been able to sleep that night, so he came to the office. He had gone for a walk, but as a creature of habit, he stopped by the office. In his mind he kept wondering how he was going to crack this case. He didn't want to bring in the FBI. But things were very strange and more women kept dying. In the middle of his reverie, the intercom in his office rang.

"Yes Harry, what's up."

"Fred I don't want to bother you with nonsense, but that cat of Mandy's is out here again."

"I'll be right out." In his mind, Fred kept hoping Roger had something for him. Fred went over to Harry's desk and saw Roger sitting on top of the desk.

"What is it Fred, is he running away from home or something?"

"I don't know, I just think he likes me and tries to visit me." Fred said this as he picked up Roger and took him to his office. As he walked away from Harry he whispered "Buddy, I hope you have good news for me." Roger nodded.

Once inside his office, Fred took out his tablet.

"I hope you have really good news for me Roger."

Roger nodded and started to type "345 Grove Street."

Fred looked at this and said "Is this where the killer lives?"

Roger nodded and motioned to write more. Fred cleared the tablet for Roger.

"Girl Alive. Killer dead. Witch dead."

Fred read this and asked "Did you kill the killer and the witch."

Roger shook his head and motioned to type.

"Demon."

Fred read this and said, "Ok, so now you're telling me there was a demon involved too?'

Roger nodded and motioned for the tablet. "Bad supernatural crap."

Fred read this and said "So, you don't believe this either, but it happened."

Roger nodded and motioned for the tablet

"Must help girl. Now."

At reading this, Fred said "You're right. I'm just so incredulous how this is wrapping up." Fred grabbed Roger and headed out his office. "Harry, call two ambulances and tell them to go to 345 Grove. I just got an anonymous tip about our killer. Jeff and Kyle, follow me in the squad car. We're heading to 345 Grove. I hope this pans out."

Fred picked up Roger and was on his way to the squad car. Roger asked Colin if he was going to come along. Colin said "No, you go ahead, there's something I have to take care of."

Once inside the car Fred tells Roger "I believe you buddy, I just gotta make it look like this was an anonymous tip." Roger nodded.

As they drove to the house, Fred told Roger "Roger this is the most insane case of my whole life. Women winding up dead missing their blood and first you tell me there was a witch and now there was a demon involved. Now, normally I'd say this is nonsense, that there's no such thing as the supernatural. But, let's look at the facts. I'm getting all my leads from a talking cat, nobody has ever seen this phenomenon of women with no blood. So, you know what? I believe you 100%

"I don't know how you can communicate with me and how you understand me speaking but you think like a cop, and you got guts Roger. I've seen you protecting Mandy in other situations and you've been slammed and rammed by this killer guy and you just get up and continue chasing him. You're out to protect the people and uphold the law just like me. I respect you more than a lot of men I've met. I just have a question. Who are you Roger?"

Roger motioned for the tablet. Fred laid it out. Roger typed "Friend."

Fred sees this and says "Buddy, right now you're my best friend in the world. You cracked this case, you got the killer and this is all coming to an end." Fred took Roger's paw and shook it.

Fred got to the house and the ambulances were already there. The other two officers got out of the car as well. Fred played it like he didn't know what to expect.

"I don't know what we're going to find in there, so keep your guns handy, this might get ugly."

The men walked up to the house and opened the door. They walked into the living room and found the woman still lying on the table, the one guy dead in the corner of the room, a pile of dust in the middle of the floor and a picture that looked like it had been set on fire and torn apart. He tested the woman's pulse.

"Ok, she's alive." He walked up to the supposed killer and test his pulse. This guy's dead, I think he's our killer. Call in the paramedics and have woman rushed to the hospital."

Paramedics came in with the gurneys "Guys, the woman is alive, let's see if we can take her to the hospital. Hopefully this guy didn't do any harm to her. The guy's dead, bring him to the station as I'm sure the lab guys are going to want to test him for prints and DNA. Tom, call up Joe, the coroner, I'm sure he's going to want to investigate this guy."

Fred set the wheels in motion for everything to be wrapped up. He figured he still had an annoying phone call to make. The phone rang a couple of times. A groggy voice sounded from the other end.

"Who is it?"

"It's me Fred. How are you doing Quincy."

"Fred, it's four in the morning, why are you calling me?"

"Because I caught the killer, because the murder spree is over."

Quincy sat up on his bed "Really? Are you sure?"

"Quincy, the town is safe again. You can start your celebration in the morning."

"You know Fred, I was only kidding about having Taylor take over. I just said that to motivate you."

"You and Dale Carnegie. Go back to sleep Quincy, everything is under control."

"Tom and Kyle, let the lab guys figure out what the hell happened here. Start filling out the reports. I think you guys got this, I'm going to sleep. I haven't slept in days over this."

"No problem Fred, this is easy."

"Yeah, I think the killer offed himself. It's possible the guilt got to him and he killed himself before he got to the girl. Who knows? The important thing is she didn't die and we got the killer. Case closed."

Fred went back to the car. Meanwhile, the paramedics were putting the woman in the ambulance. He went to his car and Roger was waiting inside.

"Hey buddy, it looked like a cyclone hit that place. We're you involved in any of that."

Roger nodded. Fred put out the tablet for him.

"Fight witch."

"So you were fighting with the witch. And then somewhere along the line the demon came along and killed the witch and the guy. Now of course, this is going to be between you and me."

Roger nodded strongly.

"The police report is going to read the guy was the killer. I'm going to play the angle he was overcome with guilt and he killed himself, couldn't take having murdered all those women.

Roger nodded again.

"Hey, I didn't see the body of the witch. Where did she go?"

Fred gave Roger the tablet. "Dust."

"Oh yeah, I saw that pile of dust in the room, I thought maybe they didn't clean up too much at this house. She turned to dust. I'm not even going to ask how that happened, this whole case is so crazy. But I take your word for it. I'm talking to a cat, how much stranger is a witch turning to dust?"

Roger nodded.

"Well buddy, I'm going to take you home, I'm sure you want to get some sleep. I sure as hell do, I haven't slept in days, just wondering how I was going to crack this case. Now, it's no longer a problem, I can sleep again. Roger I just want to say, I don't know how you did it, but thank you. You truly are a cop in a cat's body."

"You said a mouthful Fred." Fred just heard a strange meow.

CHAPTER FOURTEEN

The next morning, Lana wanted to know how things went.

"Well Roger, how did everything go last night."

"Lana it was the craziest thing I've ever seen in my life. Just be glad you weren't here. It was very dangerous and for a moment I thought I was going to be a casualty. There was also a demon who was the ugliest thing I've ever seen. But the good news is the witch is dead and this whole cycle of killings has ceased forever."

"I'm sure Lucinda is going to be happy to hear that."

"Where is Lucinda anyway?"

"I don't know. She's been in a fantasy world ever since she remembered her previous life and what really happened. I think the shock of her roaming around seven hundred years may have had a negative effect on her. I mean, to be in a fog for that long is a bit much, don't you think."

"I'll say, but it doesn't surprise me, considering how evil and selfish that witch was. She didn't care about anybody but herself. Sorry to say, the guy that slammed me against the tree and who I chased on the back of his car is dead. He was innocent, just a slave to the witch. She had him under some spell that worked in conjunction with the picture. And the picture had this demon as a prisoner sending out his own brand of evil magic. The whole thing was very sick and negative. And unfortunately, the slave to the witch is the fall guy, because people in this world don't believe in witches and demons."

In the middle of this conversation, Mandy came over to Roger.

"Roger honey, they're having a celebration about catching the serial killer on tv. Fred is going to be honored. Come watch."

"C'mon Lana, let's see what they say."

Mandy, Roger and Lana sat on the sofa. On the tv, Quincy Wells was addressing an audience at the mall plaza.

"Ladies and gentlemen, I called this tv broadcast to announce that our town is safe again. The person responsible for attacking all those women has been caught. In the process of being caught, he killed himself, so at this point, he'll never be a menace again. I want to say the success of capturing this criminal is due solely to the efforts of Captain Fred Stone, who has worked tirelessly to bring this man to justice."

At this point there was a lot of applause from the crowd. Fred looked like he hadn't slept in days and Roger was sure he would still be asleep if the mayor hadn't called this news conference.

"I would like to ask Captain Stone if he has any words to share with us."

"Thank you, Mayor Wells, and thank you citizens of Pleasant Falls. Although this case has certainly been one of the most challenging of my life, I want to thank all the men on the police force who helped bring this case to a close. I also want to say a special thank you to individuals who helped greatly with this case but are not part of the force. To you, I am truly grateful. It brings me great satisfaction to bring these horrible events to a close and that Pleasant Falls is once again the peaceful, law abiding town it has always been. And with a Mayor like Quincy Wells at the helm, we can all look to great leadership in the future."

Fred turned to Quincy and winked.

There was applause and some cheers at knowing the town was safe again.

Mandy said "You heard that Roger, Fred thanked you on tv."

"I'm just happy there are no more killings." Mandy just heard strange meows.

Quincy Wells came back on "I think we can all agree we are very lucky to have a man like Fred Stone running our police department."

Again, more applause from the crowd.

The news conference lasted another five minutes with Quincy Wells blowing his horn for re-election. Mandy shut the tv off and went to the kitchen to make herself a cup of tea. She turned to Roger "Roger, I don't know what you did, but thank you for your part in saving these women. Just like you've saved me in the past, now you're not only my hero, but you're everybody's hero, even though nobody really knows it was you."

"That's ok Mandy, we can rest peacefully again." Meowing is all Mandy heard.

"I wish I could understand you. Well, maybe someday."

Roger and Lana went to the bedroom while Mandy was

in the kitchen. At that moment Colin showed up.

"Hey Colin, you kind of disappeared last night. But thanks for your help when we really needed it."

"I have some very good news Roger, which is going to make this case even stranger."

"What happened now?"

"Well, you remember last night the blood and light coming out of the witch?"

"Yes, that vision will haunt my nightmares for nights to come."

"Well, believe it or not, that was a good thing."

"How so."

"Well, you see in order for the witch's spell to work, she needed the blood and essence of all twelve women. In the meantime, she stored these miniature versions of the women inside of herself by taking their life essence and their blood. All these women were in a sort of suspended animation inside of the witch. That's why they were in a state of not dead, but not quite alive either. Nothing final could happen until she had twelve of them. So, the light you saw coming out of the witch was their life essence as well as their blood. With the witch not being able to keep them prisoners inside of her, the essence and blood went back to the individual bodies and reverted them back to the state they were in before being captured by the witch's henchman. So, they all came back to life.

"I stuck around to make sure when their life essence came back to their bodies, there would be no problems. But it was like a homing pigeon, each life essence knew where to return to, as did the blood guided by the life essence. The women had no recollection of what happened other than they were in the hospital. Various doctors came over to check out their state and they were found to be healthy, even the shock of waking up in the hospital didn't affect them much. They truly don't remember anything."

"You are right Colin, just when I thought this case couldn't get any weirder, it just went over the top of craziness, the victims coming back to life. I'm still waiting for the tooth fairy to show up. But how are they going to keep this event under wraps?"

"Oh, it hasn't been announced. I have also been placing very strong suggestions in people's mind to leave these women alone. They don't need to suffer the trauma of being constantly besieged to speak about their experience. Especially today with all this social media nonsense."

"You mean you've been hypnotizing people."

"Well, lives are at stake here Roger. We can't risk people having their lives disrupted because of sensationalism and people trying to make financial gain. This way, these women can go back to their private lives and not suffer because of nosy people. They're being counseled as to what to say about their experience, in light of the fact that they're all young women and live in social media. They're being told to say they suffered from comatose temporary amnesia and they can't account for lost time."

"Yes, you're right. Once people catch wind of this, there's no telling what the media will do to them. They were horrible in my time, they probably haven't changed."

"No Roger, they've gotten worse."

"Well, it's the best thing you did."

At around this time, Lucinda comes into the room. She seemed kind of melancholy but trying to keep a brave face.

"Hi everybody."

"Hi Lucinda. Hey good news, just wanted to tell you,

the witch was killed last night and along with it the spell on your picture. Your picture is not going to create any problems any longer. And you don't have to fear the witch, she is dead, completely dead, saw her die myself."

"That is great news. Hopefully I won't have to walk in a fog anymore, that was probably her spell I was under."

"I'm sure you're going to feel much better now."

"But I have to ask, is there any happy ending for me. I'm still alone, away from my family, and I don't want to walk through the spirit world alone any more. What's going to happen to me? Is there any hope for a better life for me?"

Desperation was beginning to take over Lucinda, the uncertainty of the future and awareness of all the bad things that had happened to her. Colin started to speak.

"I have looked into this for you Lucinda. The only way for you to be free is if somebody that loves you would try to claim you. But since your family have thought you were lost for 700 plus years, it may take them some getting used to knowing you are still alive, in the spirit world."

"So, you're saying I'll stay alone because they probably don't believe I'm still alive and even if they did believe it, they probably have forgotten me and moved on." Colin was going to answer, but at this point Lucinda broke down crying, thinking she would be alone forever. Roger tried to give Lucinda some hope.

"Lucinda, don't cry, don't be sad. Listen, you can stay with us, you don't have to be alone. Somehow you came to us, and even though we're just two cats, an angel and Mandy, we're family, and you can be part of our family, we can do fun things together. Usually Colin and me get involved in guy talk, but now, you and Lana can have girl talk conversations, I'm sure Lana is sick of hanging around me all the time. And we're really a lot of fun, once you get to know us."

"Thank you very much noble little cat, you truly are a great detective and a great being."

"You can call me Roger."

The day went on, with Roger and Lana trying to cheer up Lucinda and tell her about this world. Conversations and exchange of knowledge went on way into the night. Lucinda felt a little better, but she was still dealing with the fact that she had been alone for over seven hundred years.

Roger suggested, "Hey, why don't we all go for a walk, take in the night air, instead of being cooped up inside. We can share some of the things we like. Actually Lucinda, you can tell us what kind of foods you like? We want you to be happy and well fed. We don't want you to go hungry. Actually, do ghosts even eat?"

"Oh noble little cat, you can be very funny."

"I told you we were a fun group. Ok, let's hit the street, c'mon, you too Colin, let's make it a whole family outing." Roger was motioning with his head to Lucinda, that this was all an act to make Lucinda feel better.

Roger, Lana, Colin and Lucinda were walking down the sidewalk and if anybody looked all they would have seen was two cats taking the night air, the other two were invisible to normal humans.

"This is actually a very nice night, very quiet and of a pleasant temperature."

All of a sudden in the distance you heard the voice of somebody singing.

"It's 3 o'clock in the morning, who the hell is singing at this hour. Hey Caruso, people are sleeping you know, they gotta get up to go a job in the morning. You know what a job is, don't you? Maybe you should try getting one and stop keeping people up at night."

Then Lucinda said "Hush noble little cat, I must listen."

The distant voice was the voice of someone who had lost all hope. He sang a song that went something like this:

My precious princess fair
Did pledge her love to me
Her beauty and her majesty
Do cast their spell on me
When winter doth arrive
Her love doth keep me warm
I love her more than life
I pray she'll be my wife

Upon hearing this, Lucinda broke out into song

My precious love and prince
So tender and so warm
You treat me like your queen
So gallant is your form
The Kings may come and go
The world will make amends
The love I have for you my friend
Will never, ever end

This caused the man who sang originally to sing with renewed energy, like his life depended on his rendition of this one song. Lucinda, upon hearing such a heartfelt rendition, replied with her version of the song, and she sang for all the world to hear. After her song, a pin point of light appeared and started to get bigger and bigger. It eventually turned into a man. It was Tranthen.

"Oh Lucinda, my darling, I have hoped against hope for so many years you would still be alive. I loved you so much, when I learned of your death, I could never marry another, even though my family encouraged me to do so. Later in death I did not see you and wondered what had happened to you. But my love for you said that someday I would find you. Recently an angel came to visit our clan and told us that if somebody loved Lucinda and went searching for her, she would be found this time."

"Tranthen, it gladdens my heart so to see you again. I had lost all hope of being found, but these kind cats helped me and kept me company while I went through a great ordeal. Eventually I remembered who I was but I was totally alone. I believe that meeting them brought you to me."

While Lucinda and Tranthen embraced and just looked into each other eyes while speaking in hushed tones, Roger was speaking to Colin.

"You know Colin, word on the street says that an angel went to visit Lucinda and Tranthen's family and told them how to find her. You wouldn't know anything about that, would you?

Colin was staring at the stars, making believe he was unaware of what was happening.

"Hello, earth to Colin, come in Colin."

"Oh, alright, I tried to tell her but then she broke down crying and you were doing such a good job of consoling her I didn't want to interrupt. I figured she would find out the truth sooner or later. I'm glad it was sooner."

"How did they know it was an angel?"

"Well, I showed up in full regalia, wings and all. I only look like a bookish librarian when I come to see you, so you can feel comfortable."

"I see."

While Roger and Colin were talking, Lucinda and Tranthen were lost in a trance of love. At one point they kissed and turned into a ball of light. Then a light from heaven touched them and started to guide the ball of light up. As the ball went up, you could hear them singing their song to each other over and over and it would get fainter and fainter as they got further and further away. At one point they were so far away you couldn't hear them anymore.

"I gotta tell you Colin, this whole case has been strange, but what just happened to Lucinda and Tranthen is definitely one for the books."

"Roger, nothing is stronger than the power of love."

Thank you for reading this book

Thank You! If you've enjoyed "Murder at the Hedge Fund", would you please take a minute to leave a review on Amazon. Even just a few sentences would be great. When you leave a review it helps others who are looking for new cozy mysteries to read, and it helps me improve the books. Plus I'd love to hear what you think.

Be sure to get your FREE e-book "Suicide in Manhattan" here:

http://bit.ly/2AEW7Hl

"Suicide in Manhattan" is a wacky romantic comedy set in the 1950s about two late bloomers who fall in love while trying to figure out life in general. A sweet clean romance.

You'll also be informed of when new books in the series are going to be released.

Thank you, Eleanor Kittering

ABOUT THE AUTHOR

In a world filled with cozy mystery writers, Eleanor Kittering saw that there was still one little nook that hadn't been filled, so, she's fulfilling that part of the female sleuth universe.

And in a world filled with all types of heroines, in this book we have one that never wanted to solve a mystery, but somehow winds up doing it, and who owns a cat that could help her but doesn't know that he can.

So please, check out how a zodiac, tarot reading housewife from New Jersey and her somewhat mystical cat find justice for the murder of her friend. .

Other Books by
Eleanor Kittering

Murder at the Art Gallery Book 1	Murder At The Art Gallery A Mandy and Roger Cozy Mystery Book 1 Eleanor Kittering
Mystery at the Pet Food Corp Book 2	Mystery At The Pet Food Corp. A Mandy and Roger Cozy Mystery Book 2 Eleanor Kittering
Murder at the Pet Spa Book 3	Murder At The Pet Spa A Mandy & Roger Cozy Mystery Book 3 Eleanor Kittering
More books on the next page	

More Books by Eleanor Kittering

Mystery at the Hedge Fund Book 4	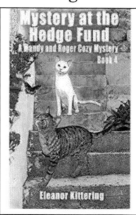
Mystery of the Zodiac Killer Book 5	
Roger and the Case of the Missing Sweater Book 6	

Made in the USA
Middletown, DE
17 December 2020